"You show so much emotion in your eyes, Agatha," Graham murmured. *"Have they ever shone with such beauty, such excitement for a man?"*

Autumn gulped. What was happening to her theory that Graham wouldn't find dowdy old Agatha attractive?

"Well?" he asked again.

His hand was warm and strong as he took her hand in his, stroking and caressing it until she could feel the heat traveling up her arm and into her face.

He was going to kiss her! Oh, hallelujah, she thought, but wouldn't Agatha push him away? She'd been waiting hours, days, a lifetime for this kiss . . . if only Agatha didn't exist!

"Agatha," Graham whispered, his lips close to hers.

"Unhand me, you cad!" she cried, then wanted to die of embarrassment. Cad? It was really too much.

"Oh, I'm sorry," Graham said quickly, moving away from her. "I—I moved too quickly."

Autumn turned away in frustration, and began stomping down the sidewalk. Why had he wanted so to kiss Agatha? Not her, Autumn, but unappealing Agatha? She wanted him to want *her*, to feel his lips on hers, to be held in those strong arms. . . . Oh, what kind of a monster had she created?

WHAT ARE *LOVESWEPT* ROMANCES?

They are stories of true romance and touching emotion. We believe those two very important ingredients are constants in our highly sensual and very believable stories in the *LOVESWEPT* line. Our goal is to give you, the reader, stories of consistently high quality that may sometimes make you laugh, sometimes make you cry, but are always fresh and creative and contain many delightful surprises within their pages.

Most romance fans read an enormous number of books. Those they truly love, they keep. Others may be traded with friends and soon forgotten. We hope that each *LOVESWEPT* romance will be a treasure—a "keeper." We will always try to publish

*LOVE STORIES YOU'LL NEVER FORGET
BY AUTHORS YOU'LL ALWAYS REMEMBER*

The Editors

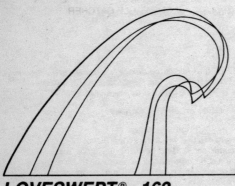

LOVESWEPT® · 162

Joan Elliott Pickart
Secrets of Autumn

BANTAM BOOKS
TORONTO · NEW YORK · LONDON · SYDNEY · AUCKLAND

SECRETS OF AUTUMN

A Bantam Book / October 1986

If you would be interested in receiving protective vinyl
covers for your Loveswept books, please write to this address
for information:

Loveswept
Bantam Books
P.O. Box 985
Hicksville, NY 11802

ISBN 0-553-21785-2

Published simultaneously in the United States and Canada

PRINTED IN THE UNITED STATES OF AMERICA

O   0 9 8 7 6 5 4 3 2 1

For BJ James who walks on her beach
while I walk in my desert . . .
and understands.

One
_____

"You're giving up what?"

"Sex."

"For a minute there, I thought you said that you're giving up sex."

"I am."

"Sure, right. The great Graham Kimble is taking on the celibate life. You're so full of bull, Cracker."

"Knock off that dopey nickname, Bish. You don't call a successful man of thirty Graham Cracker. Anyway, back to the subject. I'm giving up sex."

"I'll bite. Why?"

"It all came together for me two weeks ago on my birthday. I want to get married. I'm ready to settle down, get out of the fast lane, go for hearth and home, wife and babies."

"Fascinating. Did you flunk sophomore biology? You don't order babies out of a catalog. You're weird, Cracker. You want to get married, but you're giving up sex?"

"You don't understand."

"I'm trying, I'm trying, but you aren't making any sense."

Graham Kimble slouched back in the booth in the bar and frowned. A lock of sandy-blond hair fell over his forehead, and he impatiently pushed it back. After a minute he leaned forward again, crossing his arms on the table.

"Okay," he said, "let me try again. I made a list of every woman I've taken out in the past six months. Well, at least the names I could remember. Then I wrote down why I was attracted to them. Looks, build, sex. That's it."

"Sounds good to me," Bish said, lifting one shoulder in a shrug. "What's the problem?"

"Brains. They were all bubbleheads. I want a wife who is intelligent, so we can talk, share, be equal partners. I'm giving up sex in my relationships so I can discover the woman's mind. Beauty is now irrelevant."

"You want a smart girl who's ugly as sin? Sick."

"My vast experience has shown me that you can't have both glamour and intelligence. It's sad, but true. I've had my share of the glitzy gals."

"That's no joke."

"Hey, you do all right, Terzoni. What women see in you, I'll never know. So big deal that you drip with Italian charisma and sex appeal, have those bedroom eyes and . . . What did Marilyn say about your hair? Oh, yeah. As black as the devil's own. Lord. 'That body, that body,' Rosalie moans every time I see her. 'Tell Bish Terzoni I want his body!' Nauseating."

Bish chuckled. "Enough about my magnificent self," he said. "Let's get back to business here. You're hell-bent on getting married?"

"Yep."

"That in itself is not wise."

"You have to be fair, Bish. Just because your marriage ended in divorce doesn't mean mine will. I'm going to find the perfect woman. I want the old-fashioned type, who is willing to stay home and raise our children, tend to their needs and mine."

"You're dreaming, Cracker. There aren't any of those left, my son. They were trampled under the feet of the liberation stampede."

"How profound. And wrong. They're out there. Somewhere. I'll find her. I simply have to remember that her surface beauty is of no significance."

"Well," Bish said, "if nothing else, this is going to be interesting. Where do you plan to start looking?"

"I have no idea," Graham said, frowning again. "Where does one find a Harriet Housewife type?"

"The last of them were back in the sixties, I think. Uh-oh, here comes the ever-famous Betty Bazooms type. She's got that gleam in her eye."

"Who is it?" Graham asked, sliding down in the booth.

"I can't remember her name. Champagne?"

"Oh, Lord. Charmaine?"

A tall, well-endowed blonde in a black dress slid into the booth next to Graham and kissed him fully on the mouth.

"Hello, sweetheart," she said. "Long time no see. Hi, Bish," she added, not looking at him.

" 'Lo, Champagne," Bish said, suppressing a smile. "Would you two prefer to be alone?"

"No!" Graham said quickly. "Charmaine, how's life?"

"Fine, now that I'm with you. Whaddaya say we go to my place? I've got some great new Billy Joel tapes."

"Charmaine," Graham said, "I have very sad news."

"Oh?" she said.

"Oh?" Bish said, leaning forward.

Graham glared at Bish before redirecting his attention to Charmaine, who had managed to wiggle closer and press her voluptuous breasts against his chest. He swallowed heavily.

"Yes," he said, "I've had a slight accident. Nothing permanent, just something that will keep me out of commission for a while."

"Really?" she said, her eyes widening. "What happened?"

"What happened," Graham repeated. "What happened?"

"He was riding a horse," Bish said. "That animal had to have been going a hundred miles an hour and, lo and behold, it just stopped dead in its tracks. Certain parts of Graham's anatomy came in contact rather abruptly with the saddle horn. Get it?"

"Oh, you poor baby," Charmaine crooned. "Maybe I should fix you some chicken soup."

"That won't help," Graham said, rolling his eyes.

"Well, you *will* call me when you're recovered

from your gruesome injury, won't you?" she asked, sliding out of the booth.

"You bet," Graham said. "See ya."

"Bye, Champagne," Bish said.

"A horse?" Graham asked Bish as Charmaine wiggled away.

"She bought it, didn't she? I wonder what plans she had for that chicken soup?"

"I don't want to know. Let's get out of here."

Outside, the men hunched their shoulders against the damp, chilly fog that had rolled in to end the April day in San Francisco.

"I hope it's clear tomorrow," Bish said as they walked across the parking lot. "I'm supposed to fly to Denver to look at some property. I'd rather not have to go on a commercial flight."

"The Red Baron in his nifty little Piper Cub," Graham said. "I'll have those condo plans ready for you by next week. I swear, I'm such a superior architect I amaze myself sometimes."

"You'd better be superb, considering what you charge me. Of course, I know that it's Nancy who keeps you on the straight and narrow in that office."

"You had to mention Nancy, didn't you? She starts her vacation tomorrow. Two weeks of visiting her grandchildren, and I'm going to be lost without her."

"Are you getting a temporary?"

"Yeah, some woman Nancy knows. It'll save me the hassle of messing around with a placement service. If Nancy says she's good, that's all I need to know. I hope she can make decent coffee."

"Are you nuts, Cracker? You can't ask secretaries to do that anymore. It's not in their job description."

"It is in my office!"

"You'd better hope Nancy never decides to retire. You're in for a rude awakening. Say now, I see a potential problem here."

"What are you talking about?"

"Your car." Bish waved his hand in the direction of Graham's sports car. "I ask you, is a Ferrari a family car? No. Will it transport the wife and kiddies to the mall? No. Can you take your turn in the carpool to Little League practice? That car has got to go!"

"Like hell! I'll buy my wife a station wagon. Hey, I've thought of all these things. I'm going to be a terrific husband."

"With an ugly wife."

"Knock it off. Can you see me married to Charmaine?"

"She'd have her moments. Champagne is very well put together. She's also a ding-dong."

"I rest my case. Call me when you get back from Denver."

"Count on it. I'll want a full report on your progress. Good luck, Cracker."

"Don't call me that!"

"I've called you Cracker since you were ten years old!"

"Well, I'm thirty now. This is the turning point of my life, a time of maturity and discovery."

"Personally, I think you're going through a midlife crisis slightly early. You can't wake up one morning and decide to get married."

"You did."

"Yeah, well, there were extenuating circumstances. Forget it. That's old news. Just make sure you know what you're doing, Graham. This is a helluva big step you're contemplating here."

"I realize that, but it's time, Bish. I'm sick of the singles scene. I want a home, a wife, kids. I really do. Damn, it's cold out here. See you when you get back."

"Okay," Bish said, and slid behind the wheel of his Mercedes.

The pair drove in the same direction for several miles, then Bish turned to the west and the Pacific Heights area, where his majestic home was located in that exclusive neighborhood. Graham's destination was Nob Hill, also exclusive and affluent, but his home was a large apartment on the twelfth floor of a high rise.

Inside his sprawling living room, Graham tossed his jacket onto a chair, then immediately snatched it up again.

"Not good," he muttered. "A wife would be bugged by a slob. I've got to get my act together. Damn, I wish I knew what Charmaine had been planning on doing with that chicken soup!"

Autumn Stanton inserted the key in the lock and stepped into the plushly furnished reception area. After dropping her purse on the desk, she flicked on the lights and poked her head inside the door of the inner office.

Classy, she thought. The furniture was of the finest quality, and the building itself was in the high-rent business district. Graham Kimble was apparently doing all right for himself. According to her aunt Nancy, Kimble was the boy wonder of the architectural world, but Aunt Nancy had a mother complex about him. Autumn had certainly heard enough about Mr. Wonderful in the three years her aunt had worked for him.

Autumn glanced at her watch, then went into the small bathroom off the reception area to check her appearance. She jumped in surprise at her own reflection, then scrutinized it critically.

Good, she thought. She looked terrible. Her strawberry-blond hair was pulled back into a tight, slightly lopsided bun. Her heart-shaped face was devoid of makeup, and her ivory skin had a sickly pallor due to the olive-green suit she was wearing. Olive green was definitely not her color. Although her eyes were still large and green and her lips full and nicely shaped, she fervently hoped they would go unnoticed. The suit itself was delightfully grim. It was a size too big, which caused it to droop in strange places, and it camouflaged her curvaceous figure. The shoes were super. They were black oxfords with chunky heels that added very little height to her five feet four inches.

Remembering her glasses, she hurried back to her desk, dug them out of her purse, and shoved them onto her nose. The heavy black frames with the clear glass weighed a ton, but they were just the touch she needed to complete her dismal ensemble.

Autumn uncovered the typewriter, then glanced at a note on the desk. It was the list of instructions her aunt had said she would leave in regard to being a top-notch secretary for darling Graham.

"Make the coffee," Autumn read aloud. "Make the coffee? Brother!"

She stomped to the far side of the room and discovered that her clumpy shoes were great for expressing dissatisfaction as they thudded against the thick carpet.

Poor Aunt Nancy, Autumn mused as she prepared the coffee. She had had to talk a blue streak to get her aunt to agree to this plan. No harm would come to Nancy's precious Graham, Autumn had declared over and over. His office would run like clockwork, Autumn would gather the data she needed, and Nancy would have a lovely vacation. Everybody would be happy.

"You know I can type like a whiz, Aunt Nancy," Autumn had said.

"Yes, dear, but Graham is extremely busy, and needs someone who can take care of him, anticipate his needs."

"I'll anticipate my little heart out! Oh, Aunt Nancy, please! This is the final example for my dissertation. I'm this far away from my doctorate in psychology. My dissertation is going to be brilliant, but I need one more example. Just one!"

"Well—"

"Haven't you enjoyed hearing about my findings in the past two months?" Autumn had asked. "When I went into that seedy bar dressed as a nun, those construction workers were pussycats, paragons of politeness. Then, when I went back in that tight red satin number, I heard words I didn't know existed and had twenty-seven offers in thirty-four minutes."

"Shame on those young men," Nancy had clucked.

"And," Autumn had continued, beginning to pace the floor, "when I padded myself to look seven months pregnant, ten men—and three women—offered me a seat on the bus. When I got on in tight jeans and a sweater, heavy makeup, and a wad of gum in my mouth, no one moved. One more example, Aunt Nancy, that's all I need. Combined with the extensive research I've done on women in society dating back to the turn of the century, I'll be ready to go for my doctorate. Please?"

"But to play a trick on Graham isn't very nice."

"It's not a trick. Well, it sort of is, but he still gets an efficient secretary out of the deal. The first week I'll be prim, proper, frumpy Agatha, who is strictly business and very unattractive. The second week I'll be Autumn, beautifully dressed and quite friendly."

"I don't know, Autumn," Nancy had said.

"Aunt Nancy, my dissertation is based on the theory that men are remarkably like their fathers and grandfathers. They want to protect their women, cherish them, keep them from harm. The men haven't changed in our society, the women have. According to my research, Graham Kimble will treat Agatha with respect and dignity, a strict employer/employee relationship. But he'll see 'Autumn' as a woman first, and treat her accordingly."

"All right," Nancy had said, throwing up her hands, "I give up. I'll worry myself into an early grave, but I give up."

"Thank you!" Autumn had said, hugging her

tightly. "Thank you! I love you dearly. I'm going to be Dr. Autumn Stanton!"

And now, here she was, ready to put part A of her plan into effect. Agatha had arrived!

Autumn sat in the chair behind her desk, folded her hands primly in her lap, and waited. A few minutes later a man entered and strode quickly past her into the inner office.

"Morning, Nancy," he called.

Autumn pushed her glasses up on her nose and kept silent.

The man returned, walked to the coffeepot, picked it up, then stopped. With the pot in one hand, a mug in the other, he turned slowly to face Autumn.

"You're not Nancy," he said. "Oh, Lord, I forgot. She started her vacation today. You're her friend? Oh, I'm Graham Kimble. You're Nancy's friend?"

"Miss Agatha Stanton," she said, getting to her feet and extending her hand. Oh, dear heaven above, she thought wildly, Graham Kimble was gorgeous! Aunt Nancy had always said he was good-looking, but Autumn had assumed she'd exaggerated. What Kimble did for that perfectly cut brown suit was sinful. Not to mention his thick, sandy blond hair and dark brown eyes. And his shoulders were so broad, his legs so long. Was her hand trembling? Dammit, it was! But that was okay. It fit Agatha's image of insecurity.

Graham looked at the coffeepot, the mug, then set them both back on the counter. He walked to the front of Autumn's desk, blinked once slowly, and took her hand.

"Well!" he said a bit too loudly. "Welcome aboard, Agatha. May I call you Agatha?"

"Certainly, sir," she said. Such a strong hand, she mused. And warm, very warm. Oh, for Pete's sake, she was acting ridiculous. Graham Kimble was nothing more than an average, run-of-the-mill, beautiful, incredible, unbelievable member of the male species. No big deal. But oh-h-h, what a hunk of stuff!

"Have you found everything you need?" he asked, releasing her hand.

"Yes, thank you. My . . . friend Nancy left me a very detailed list of instructions. I assure you, Mr. Kimble, that I'm a highly efficient secretary, and will be an asset to you during the length of my stay."

"I'm sure you will," he muttered, walking back to the coffeepot. "Call me Graham."

"If you prefer," Autumn said. "Was there something you wished me to do for you, Mr. . . . Graham?"

"What? Oh, no. Not right now. I'll let you know." He strode quickly into his office.

Autumn sank into her chair and pressed her hand to her forehead to check her temperature. What in the world was the matter with her? She'd been knocked totally off kilter by Graham Kimble! She'd dated plenty of handsome, well-built men. But darn it, there was just something about Graham Kimble, a blatant sexuality and virility. She had to get a grip on herself. She was here for a purpose, and it did not include fainting dead away on the floor whenever her boss entered the room! The bum had even smelled good, a fresh, soapy aroma with the hint of a woodsy after-shave. He really didn't play fair!

Autumn pushed her glasses back up onto her nose and frowned.

Graham took a sip of his coffee and shook his head. Was that woman, that Agatha person, for real? he wondered. Did a woman actually get up in the morning and dress like that? Apparently so, but good Lord, she was unattractive! She did have a soft, pretty hand with slender fingers. And her eyes were a lovely shade of green. But overall she looked so plain and old-fashioned.

Graham straightened abruptly in his chair, nearly spilling his coffee. Old-fashioned? Yes! She looked like she'd been transported from his mother's era. Was Agatha a modern, liberated woman who just didn't have a lick of fashion sense, or was she an honest-to-goodness transplant from the Victorian age, a Harriet Housewife type? She sure as hell wasn't a Betty Bazooms. Could it be that he'd lucked out, had a hearth-and-home type dumped right into his lap? But good Lord, the thought of sitting across the breakfast table every morning from Agatha was depressing. The morning after a night of what? No, by damn, sex was not entering into this. He had to keep his priorities straight. He wanted an old-fashioned wife! First order of business was to check out Miss Agatha Stanton a bit more.

"Agatha," he said into the intercom, "would you bring me the Terzoni file, please?"

"Right away, sir," she said. All she had to do was find it!

The filing cabinet was in perfect order, and a minute later Autumn walked into Graham's office. He was definitely scrutinizing her as she approached his desk, she realized, but there was no readable expression on his face.

"Thank you," he said, accepting the file. "Have a seat while I look this over." His grandmother wore shoes like that! he thought.

He stood up and walked to the large drafting table by the floor-to-ceiling windows. He pretended to compare the blueprints on the table to the information in the file, while he was, in actuality, watching Agatha Stanton. She had sat in the chair in front of his desk and crossed her legs in a seemingly automatic gesture. The next instant she whipped her foot back to the floor, her heavy shoe landing with a thud on the carpet. There she sat, ramrod stiff, eyes front, hands folded in her lap. And her glasses were sliding slowly down her nose.

"This project is coming along great," Graham said, returning to his chair. "So, tell me about yourself, Agatha."

"I'm twenty-six, single, and own a very cute cat," she said pleasantly.

"And you're a friend of Nancy's?"

"Yes, we're very close."

"Do you have any hobbies?" Graham asked, rolling a pencil back and forth on the top of the desk with his finger.

"My spare time is mainly taken up with my studies and internship."

"Oh?" He sat up straighter. "Tell me more."

"I'm working on my doctorate in psychology. I'm preparing my dissertation now, and completing the required number of hours training with a doctor on actual cases."

All right! Graham mentally cheered. A superbrain! But wait a minute. If she'd knocked herself out for that degree, she'd never give up her career in exchange for diapers and bottles.

"You're very career-oriented, I take it," he said, frowning slightly.

"To a point. As a psychologist I could set my own pace as to how many clients I'd wish to take on. If I ever had, for example, a husband and children, I would balance everything so that no one area suffered. But that's all conjecture, because I have yet to get my degree."

She was getting better by the minute, Graham thought. This was unbelievable!

Autumn was perplexed. Why was such a supposedly busy man like Graham Kimble sitting around chatting? He must be the nosy type, because he sure as heck couldn't be interested in her as a woman. Graham would definitely prefer the flash-and-dash gals.

What would it be like, she wondered, to be pulled against Graham's chest, held tightly by those arms, as he lowered his head to bring his lips to hers? Delicious. No doubt about it. Graham Kimble was one very, very sexy man.

A funny sensation tingled in the pit of Autumn's stomach, and she shifted in her chair. She pushed her glasses up, cleared her throat, and plastered a pleasant expression on her face.

"Don't those glasses bother you?" Graham

asked. "I mean, they're very nice, but they don't seem to stay in one spot."

"I know," she said, frowning. "They're a bit heavy. They make my teeth ache."

"Pardon?"

"It's very strange." She pressed her fingertips to her cheeks. "My teeth nerves must be connected to my nose nerves or something. My teeth are killing me."

"Why don't you take your glasses off? You'd be more comfortable, and it's a shame to hide those lovely green eyes. You really do have beautiful eyes, Agatha."

"What?" What was this malarkey? she asked herself. Graham wasn't supposed to have noticed Agatha's eyes, let alone compliment them. Especially not in that low, rumbly voice.

"It's true," he said. He really did like her eyes, he thought. They were large, and a unique shade of green. He wanted to see them without the goggles. "So take off the glasses and take pity on your teeth."

"I don't think that's a terrific idea. I can't see all that well without them. Would you like me to put that file away?"

"No, I need it."

"Well," she said, getting to her feet, "I must get back to my desk. Was there anything else?"

"Not at the moment," he said. He shrugged out of his jacket, and draped it over the back of his chair.

Autumn's shoes seemed suddenly nailed to the floor as she watched Graham undo the buttons on the cuffs of his shirt. He rolled the sleeves up, revealing muscular forearms covered in a smattering of blond hair. The simple gesture of folding soft, expensive material in a slow, steady motion took on an unearthly sensuous quality, and Autumn's gaze was riveted on his arms.

"Agatha?"

"What?" she yelled, jumping in surprise.

"Is something wrong?"

"No. No, of course not. I'm going to my desk. Bye." She left the room as quickly as her shoes allowed her to.

Safely back at her desk, Autumn sank onto her chair and pulled off her glasses. She pinched the bridge of her nose, then clicked her teeth together several times to see if they were going to crumble into dust. The glasses were a pain, literally. And Graham Kimble? He was, to quote her teenage neighbor, awesome. He was also a threat to her mental equilibrium.

Her reaction to Graham was totally unlike her. She knew she was pretty, and enjoyed her attractiveness, but she didn't flaunt it. She had as full and exciting a social life as time allowed and had postponed considering any serious relationship until after obtaining her coveted doctorate degree.

Never in all her years of keeping company with the male sex had she been jolted the way she had been by Graham Kimble. There was just something about him that rattled her right down to her socks. Even dressed in her ridiculous get-up, she'd been acutely aware of her own femininity. He was so potently male that she wanted to shout for joy because she was soft and curved where he was hard and rugged. They were counterparts, man to woman, and the implications of that were delicious and intriguing. It was also slightly frightening to think a man could have such a disconcerting effect on her. She had to get herself under control! Now!

She tugged decisively on the lapels of her jacket, poked her glasses back into place, and picked up the list of instructions furnished by Aunt Nancy. It was standard, containing the usual dos and don'ts regarding answering the telephone and taking messages, the necessity for error-free typing, on and on. When she got to the bottom of the piece of paper, however, Autumn's eyes widened.

"Monday," her aunt had written, "remind Graham to get a haircut. Tuesday, remind Graham to pick up his shirts at the laundry. Wednesday, remind Graham to make an appointment to have his car serviced."

Autumn smacked the paper onto the desk and pursed her lips. What was she, his mother? A grown man didn't know when he needed a haircut? Personally, she liked it the length it was, the way it curled slightly as it fell over the top of his collar. But she was a secretary, not a baby-sitter. Aunt Nancy had spoiled Graham rotten. Autumn would choke before she told him to get a haircut!

Graham tapped the end of his pencil against his chin and stared at the ceiling. Agatha Stanton, he thought. Even her name was old-fashioned. She was intelligent, had dreams of a husband and children, and would not place her career above the needs of her family. She was perfect. Love didn't have to enter into the picture, because he wasn't all that convinced it existed. Compatibility was the key, mutual interests in raising a family, possessing similar goals and values. Yes, he admitted, sex was important, but there was more to marriage than just the physical.

Making love with Agatha Stanton? How did old-fashioned girls behave in bed? Enough of that. He was getting ahead of himself. He had to retrain his brain to appreciate a woman for her intelligence, and the hell with her looks. Not that Agatha was unspeakably ugly. Her eyes were sensational and her lips looked very kissable. She was pretty in a blah sort of way. The clothes, though, were really the pits.

"Mr. . . . um . . . Graham," her voice came over the intercom. "Mr. Terzoni is on line one."

Graham punched the button on the telephone and snatched up the receiver.

"Bish?"

"Hey, Cracker, how's your wound?"

"My what?"

"From the horse. You must have an incredible ability to endure pain."

"Yeah, I'm tough. Are you flying to Denver?"

"Just walking out the door, but the suspense is killing me. Have you thought of where to start looking for the future Mrs. Kimble?"

"I think," Graham began, then lowered his voice, "she may have been delivered to me by a higher power. The secretary Nancy got for me is a real candidate, Bish."

"Ugly as hell, huh?"

"No, not that bad, but far removed from what I'm

accustomed to. She's very intelligent, and plans to balance her career with husband and kids."

"You found all that out already? What did you do, put her under a bare light bulb and grill her?"

"No. It calls for finesse, idle chitchat. So far, all systems are go."

"What's her name?"

"Agatha."

"Lord."

"It's an old-fashioned name for an old-fashioned woman," Graham said, nodding decisively. "I'm telling you, Bish, I'm really on to something here."

"Well, good luck, Cracker. I'll call you for an update the minute I get back."

"See ya, Bish," he said. "And don't call me Cracker!" he added to the dial tone.

Humming under his breath, Graham got back to work and was soon deeply engrossed in his project.

Autumn filled her coffee cup, then glanced idly into Graham's office. Her breath caught in her throat when she saw him sitting at the drafting table. The sun was streaming in the window, glinting off his golden hair and highlighting the strong, handsome planes of his face.

Darn it, she thought. He was, he really was the most beautiful man she had ever seen.

Two

Fifteen minutes later Autumn had just finished some filing when Graham walked out of his office.

"Agatha," he said, stopping at her desk.

"Yes, sir?"

"I need these figures typed as part of a report for Bish Terzoni. My handwriting isn't terrific, so if you can't read it, ask me what it says. There's an example of the format we use in this file. Oh, and make a carbon copy for our records, please. Any questions?"

"No, it looks clear enough. I'll get started."

"Do your teeth still hurt? I think there's some aspirin around here somewhere. I really hate to think that you're in pain."

"You do?" she said, smiling at him. "That's very considerate of you."

"I'm a nice guy," he said, grinning.

How dare he smile like that! Autumn thought irrationally. It was the first smile he'd given her, and it spread across his face like sunshine itself, finally settling in his fudge-dark eyes. Her heart was doing funny little flip-flops, and her pulse was racing. Graham Kimble cheated, she told herself. With everything else he'd been dished out, he had a hundred-watt smile to boot. It just wasn't fair!

He placed his hands flat on the desk and leaned toward her.

"Those frames are very heavy," he said. "Have you ever considered contact lenses?"

"No," she said, and was positive that her voice had squeaked.

"Do you mind?" he asked, his voice low. He slowly lifted his hands and drew the glasses from her face. Look at those eyes! he thought. Fantastic! A man could drown in that sea of green. And her face. Everything softened without the glasses. Good Lord, she was pretty. Not glamorous, but wholesome, fresh. She did have the appearance of someone just getting over the flu, but . . . "Doesn't that feel better?" he asked.

"Much," she said, clicking her teeth together. "I guess I could see without them if I squinted."

"Why don't you try it?" He handed her the glasses. "I have to say this again, Agatha. You really do have beautiful eyes."

"So do you," she said, gazing up at him. Oh, somebody tell her she hadn't said that! That hadn't been Agatha or Autumn talking. It had been a dim-wit! She'd never said such an adolescent thing in her life! What was next—would she start drooling on his shirt front? What in heaven's name was the matter with her?

"Well, I . . . Thank you for the compliment," Graham said. "I'd better get back to work," he added, and walked back into his office.

Autumn rolled her eyes in disgust at her behavior, then picked up the paper that needed typing. She would produce a picture-perfect report. Agatha was once more in control! She'd keep one ear tuned in case Graham came out of his office, then she would squint as she typed. At least she didn't have to wear those glasses anymore. Imagine Graham being concerned because her nose nerves were connected to her teeth nerves. Wasn't that just the sweetest thing? And for years men had been telling her she had beautiful eyes, but there was just something special about the way Graham said it.

"That's it!" Autumn said under her breath. "Type, for Pete's sake."

Graham slid onto his stool and listened to the sound of the typewriter coming from the outer office. Agatha was fast, he thought with approval. He was glad she'd listened to him about taking off those glasses. He really didn't like the idea of her being in pain, having every tooth in her head aching. Agatha needed someone to watch over her, keep her from harm.

Strange sentiments for him, he mused. He actually felt a sense of protectiveness toward her. But she just seemed so damn innocent and vulnerable, so out of place in today's world. Agatha Stanton was definitely an old-fashioned girl. The thing was, what did a guy do with one of those? Take her to dinner? That was safe enough. Everyone had to eat. Dancing? In those combat boots she wore? No, guess not. Night clubs? The comedians got a bit raunchy with their jokes sometimes. Sports? Agatha screaming for the winning team? Not hardly.

"I need a handbook on this," he muttered. Okay, intellectual stuff. Lectures, Shakespearean plays, museums. Was that fun? That was boring as hell! Well, he couldn't have his cake and eat it, too. He was going to have to make some sacrifices in order to marry the kind of woman he wanted as his wife. He'd had his share of the party scene, the good times, and he'd live off his memories. He couldn't expect to have everything his own way.

He had to get organized, he decided. Since he didn't have the foggiest notion as to what he was doing, he'd better formulate some kind of plan. Slow and easy was the key phrase, or he'd scare Agatha to death. He'd ask her to lunch. Great. There were times when he amazed himself with his own brilliance!

At that moment the telephone rang, and Agatha announced over the intercom that Mr. Fisher was on line one. It was nearly an hour later before Graham could get off the phone and go ask Agatha to lunch.

Autumn looked up from the page she was proof-reading and saw Graham hesitate in the doorway, then walk toward her. Her heart did a strange little tap dance at the sight of him, at the lithe, easy way he moved, the way his shirt stretched across his broad shoulders and his slacks hugged his narrow hips and muscled thighs. Her gaze swept upward to meet Graham's dark eyes as he stopped in front of her desk.

Neither spoke. Seconds ticked by as they stared at each other. A tingling sensation started in the pit of Autumn's stomach and traveled through her, showing itself as a warm flush on her cheeks.

Graham cleared his throat roughly. "Agatha," he said, shoving his hands into his pockets, "would you have lunch with me today?"

Sure, Autumn thought dreamily. Lunch, dinner, then home to her bed, where they'd make mad, passionate love until dawn. "No!" she said much too loudly, straightening in her chair. "Absolutely not!"

"Why not?" he asked, his tawny eyebrows knitting together in a frown.

"Because . . ." she began, then asked herself, Because why? Because she wanted to know if there were blond curls on that luscious chest? Oh, good grief! "Because I have to answer the phone," she blurted out.

He smiled, a dazzling smile, a bone-melting smile, and Autumn silently groaned.

"We'll just flip on the answering machine," he said. "No problem. What do you say?"

Yes! No! Why would a man like Graham Kimble want to take Agatha to lunch? Autumn wondered. It didn't make sense, *and* it was not the behavior she had expected. Darn it, why was he doing this? Well, only one way to find out.

"Why?" she asked. If he whipped an "I want to

get to know you better" number on her, she'd scream!

"I want to get to know you better," he said.

"Oh, good Lord." She pressed her hand to her forehead. "I can't believe this!"

"Look," he said, "there's a nice, quiet place around the corner that has great seafood. We'll walk over, have a quick lunch, then come right back. Okay?"

"I . . . I guess so."

"Great. Twelve o'clock," he said, then turned and strode into his office.

Autumn watched him leave, then snapped her mouth closed as she realized it was open. Damn the man! What was this, National Take a Frump to Lunch Day? Why in the world would he want to go anywhere with Agatha? She had to calm down, think this through. Graham adored Aunt Nancy, and Agatha was Nancy's friend. Check. He was simply being nice, trying to make Agatha feel comfortable in her role as his temporary secretary. Check. He'd said himself that they'd have a quick lunch, then come right back. It was a gesture of kindness on his part because of his fondness for Nancy. Check. Okay, everything was under control.

Autumn patted her lopsided bun, let out a sigh of relief, and resumed her proofreading.

This was ridiculous! Graham grumbled silently as he stared out the window. Agatha had acted like he'd asked her to go to bed with him, instead of out to lunch. Old-fashioned women were weird! What did she think he was going to do? Ravish her on top of a table in a crowded restaurant? What did she look like underneath that marine tent she was wearing? No, dammit, it didn't matter. He was interested in her intelligence, her outlook and values.

"Wonderful," he mumbled. His attitude was slipping. But hell, this was going to be hard work! He'd pleaded his case like a lawyer for a simple walk around the corner and some lunch. It would probably take an act of Congress to get her into his car!

"Patience, Kimble," he muttered under his breath. "You can handle this. Look at it as a growing experience. Ah, hell!"

With a snort, Graham slid back onto his stool and forced himself to concentrate on the drawings for Bish.

To Autumn's amazement the remainder of the morning passed quickly. The telephone rang constantly, and a huge stack of mail was delivered. Following the instructions on Aunt Nancy's list, Autumn opened each envelope, paper-clipped the contents to it, and placed it all in a basket on the corner of her desk. Just before noon she stood to go freshen her makeup, only to plop down again in a dejected heap as she remembered she had no makeup to freshen. A few minutes later Graham came out of his office, shrugging into his jacket.

"All set?" he asked as he flipped on the answering machine.

"Certainly," she said, not looking directly at him as she got to her feet. There was no way, she vowed, that she was going to gaze into those eyes of his again. The effect Graham Kimble had on her was ludicrous. Eyes were eyes, for mercy's sake, but for some dumb reason those yummy dark pools of Graham's totally unbalanced her.

Suddenly the door opened, and an attractive blond woman in a clinging blue silk dress swooped in.

"Graham," she said. She circled his neck with her arms and kissed him on the mouth. "How marvelous to see you. I just stopped by to visit Daddy, but he's all tied up in a meeting."

"Hello, Joyce," Graham said, pulling her arms from his neck. "I'd like to chat, but we're on our way out the door."

"We?" Joyce asked, scanning the office, her gaze not even lingering on Autumn. "Is Bish here?"

"No, he's in Denver," Graham said. "Agatha and I were just leaving for lunch."

"Who?"

"Agatha Stanton," Autumn said, extending her hand.

"Oh," Joyce said, shaking hands absently as she stared at Autumn. "I'm Joyce St. James."

"Charmed," Autumn said, smiling sweetly. "Don't allow us to keep you, Miss St. James. I'm sure you have a set time for lunch like the rest of us."

"I'm free until my tennis lesson," she said, appearing slightly confused.

"And you mustn't be late," Graham said. "Those tennis coaches are sticklers for punctuality. Aren't you training with Pierre Whoever, Joyce?"

"Yes," she said, sighing. "He's so wonderful.

What that man does for a pair of tennis shorts is incredible. Of course, he's not nearly as handsome as you are, Graham."

"I can't compete with a guy who speaks French," Graham said. "Well, see you, Joyce."

"What? Oh, well, all right. I guess you have business to discuss with Abigail over lunch."

"Agatha," Graham and Autumn said in unison.

"Will you call me, sweetie?" Joyce asked, trailing a manicured fingernail down Graham's cheek.

"You bet. Bye."

"Ta-ta," she said, gliding out the door.

"Damn," Graham muttered, then turned his head slowly to look at Autumn. "That was Joyce," he said lamely. "Her father owns a company that has offices in this building. She drops by once in a while to say hello and . . . stuff."

"That's nice," Autumn said. And Joyce had plenty of "stuff" to say hello with, she added silently. Joyce St. James was a little rich girl who had probably never worked a day in her life. And Graham was certainly no stranger to the sultry witch. He even knew who her tennis coach was! The pattern fit her previously gathered data perfectly. Then why wasn't she thrilled? Oh, forget it. She was hungry, that was all.

"Agatha, let's go!" Graham said gruffly.

"Of course, sir," she said, preceding him out the door.

"It's Graham!" he yelled, making her jump. "Sorry," he said. "Joyce gets on my nerves."

"She does?"

"Absolutely," he said quickly as he locked the

door. "She's a bubblehead. Just chatters on about nothing of consequence."

"She's very beautiful," Autumn said.

No joke, Graham thought as they stepped into the elevator. Joyce also had a cabin cruiser with a water bed. "She's attractive, I suppose," he said. "If you like that type. Personally, I prefer a woman who can carry on an intelligent conversation."

Bull! Autumn thought. Who was he trying to kid? She was sure that a virile man like Graham would be only too happy to take what Joyce blatantly offered. On the other hand, was Graham so sensitive that he realized Agatha must have felt inferior next to Joyce and was trying to bolster her self-esteem? Wasn't that nice? The playboys she'd met were so wrapped up in themselves they'd never even think of such an act of kindness. Well, it all came back to the fact that she was Nancy's friend. He certainly had no personal interest in Agatha Stanton!

The sun had ducked behind a cloud and shadows fell across the sidewalk, which was crowded with people on their way to lunch. The clumping sound of Autumn's heavy shoes was drowned out by the mingling of dozens of voices. Graham rested his hand on her elbow and guided her through the throng.

"The misty city of love," he said as they turned the corner. "The city . . ."

"Of the sea," Autumn finished for him.

"You know that poem?" he asked, surprised, as he pulled open the restaurant door.

"It's one of my favorites," she said, smiling up at him.

The smile was shared as their eyes met. Again, Autumn was lost in Graham's brown eyes, and again the tingling sensation crept insistently throughout her.

"Table for two, sir?" a voice asked.

"What?" Graham said, spinning around to face the hostess. "Oh, yes, for two, please." Her eyes were sensational! he thought. Like the sea, or emeralds. Did they turn smoky when she was filled with desire? Agatha desiring a man? Aching to be touched, kissed, consumed by a man? Agatha? Were there hidden fires of passion beneath that cool, drab exterior? "Somehow, I doubt it," he muttered dismally.

"Pardon?" Autumn said.

"Nothing. Just thinking out loud."

"Table for two," the hostess said. "This way, please."

Oh, no! Autumn thought with despair as they were led to a corner table. The only light seemed to be from a candle in the center of the table. Candlelight, for Pete's sake! It would flicker over Graham's handsome face, dance through the silky strands of his thick hair, and cast a golden glow that would encompass them both and push the remaining people in the room into oblivion.

And it did.

From the moment Autumn sat down across from Graham and saw the candlelight work its magic, she was lost. And furious. A section of her mind was totally disgusted with her behavior with Graham Kimble. She knew it wasn't because she had gotten caught up in her role of Agatha. No, it was Graham, and she didn't like it, not one little bit.

But the rest of her was melting like ice cream on a hot stove. As every inch of Graham's magnificent torso seemed to be magnified in the romantic setting, Autumn became that much more aware of her own femininity. Her breasts seemed to swell within her lacy bra, and a coiling heat settled deep within her. Her imagination skittered to visions of Graham reaching for her, pulling her against him and kissing her. Oh, yes, just kissing the living daylights out of her. Sweet, sweet bliss.

"Do you know what you want?" Graham asked, scanning the menu.

"You'd better believe it," she said, staring off into space.

"Me too."

She snapped out of her reverie. "What?"

"Lobster salad. It's delicious."

"Oh. Of course. I'll have lobster salad as well. I adore lobster salad."

Graham frowned at her slightly, then placed their orders while Autumn carefully spread her napkin in her lap.

"Agatha," Graham said as the waiter walked away, "do I make you nervous?"

"Nervous? Don't be silly. Well, maybe just a little."

"Why?"

"Why? Well, you see, Graham, you're not quite what I'm accustomed to. Agatha lives . . . I mean, I live a very quiet life, concentrating on my studies. You live, no doubt, in what is referred to as the fast lane. We have absolutely nothing in common, so it's a bit difficult to think of a topic of conversation over lunch." Not bad, she decided. That little spiel had sounded perfectly reasonable.

"On the contrary," he said, smiling. "I know exactly what we can discuss."

"Oh?"

"You."

"I already told you about myself."

"Not everything. Do you have family, brothers and sisters?"

Keep the lies simple, she told herself, or you'll trip yourself up later for sure. "A cousin my age named Autumn," she said.

"Pretty name."

"Autumn is extremely attractive." How conceited! Oh, well.

"And your parents?"

"They're gone." To the south of France on vacation. According to their postcards, they were having a fabulous time.

"I'm sorry."

"About what?"

"Your parents, about your being alone except for a cousin."

"Don't give it another thought," she said, patting his hand. Oh, great, she thought. Now she was getting a guilty conscience. The last thing she needed was Graham feeling sorry for poor orphaned Agatha. In reality Autumn came from a wealthy, warm, fun-loving family that consisted of her parents, an older brother she loved to pieces, and oodles of relatives in every shape and size.

"Here's our lunch," Graham said.

"Thank goodness," Autumn mumbled.

They ate in silence for several minutes as they took the sharp edge off their appetites.

"What made you decide to become a psychologist?" Graham asked finally.

"Everything about human beings fascinates me," Autumn said, smiling brightly. "We're marvelously complex creatures and, consequently, confuse ourselves at times. I'll have the opportunity to get people back on the right track. It's a tremendous challenge. I like history, too. It's so exciting to learn about the past that has helped shape today. At this very minute, we're creating history that will have an effect on the future."

"I never thought of it like that before," Graham said. "It's a very valid point."

"Do you know," she said, leaning slightly toward him, "that when Juan Manuel de Ayala discovered San Francisco Bay in 1775, it had gone undetected by ships sailing the coast for over two hundred years? Think about what he must have felt when he sailed the *San Carlos* through the entrance to the bay and— Why are you smiling?"

Graham covered her hand with his on top of the table. "Because your eyes are shining with excitement and look like precious gems," he said in a husky voice. "You show a great deal of your emotions in your eyes, Agatha. Have they ever shone like that for a man?" Her hand was so soft, so small beneath his, he thought, stroking her wrist gently with his thumb. She needed protecting from anything less than the most tender touch. He was sure no man had brought that glimmer of excitement to her eyes. "Well?" he asked.

"Well what?" she said. His hand was warm and

strong, she mused. The heat was traveling up her arm and across her breasts. There were calluses on his palm, yet his touch was gentle. Graham's hands would speak of strength tempered with care when they reached for her.

"Agatha, do you have a lover?" he asked, loudly enough for several heads to turn in his direction.

"How dare you!" she exclaimed, snatching her hand away. The nerve of the man, asking her such a question! He had fired her temper and deserved a slap across the face. But wait a minute! She wasn't Autumn, she was Agatha. How would sweet, inno- cent, frumpy Agatha react to such audacity?

"I feel faint," she said, slumping back in her chair and rolling her eyes.

"Agatha!" He jumped to his feet and hurried to her side. He circled her shoulders with his arm and patted her cheek. "Are you really going to faint? Oh, Lord, what have I done? Let's get you outside and into the fresh air."

"All right," she said, giving the remaining lob- ster salad a yearning glance as she got to her feet.

Graham tossed some money onto the table, then tucked Autumn close to his side as he led her across the room and out the door.

So strong, she thought. And he smelled so good. The fainting routine definitely had something going for it.

"Here," he said, urging her to sit on a nearby bench. "Better?"

"Yes, I think so."

"I'm really very sorry," he said, sitting down next to her and cradling her hand in both of his. "I know that was a very rude question to ask you. I don't know, Agatha. I've never met anyone like you before, and I suddenly felt very protective, like maybe you might be involved with someone who wouldn't appreciate how special you are."

"Special?" she repeated, gazing up at him. That wasn't right! Graham Kimble was supposed to treat Agatha simply as a temporary employee, not see her as something special.

"Very special," he said, smiling at her gently.

"There's no man in my life, Graham," she said softly. "There was once, but he resented the time I spent studying. I think he felt threatened by my intelligence."

"Then he wasn't much of a man," Graham said, leaning his head slowly toward hers. He wanted—needed—to kiss that soft, lovely mouth!

He was going to kiss her! Autumn thought wildly. Glory be and raise the flag, he was going to kiss her! She didn't care diddly that tons of people were tromping by on the sidewalk. She'd been waiting hours, days, a lifetime, for this kiss. But Agatha would have a conniption fit. Oh, how she wished Agatha would take a hike!

"Agatha," Graham murmured, his lips only a breath away from hers.

"Unhand me, you cad," she cried, jumping to her feet. Cad? she repeated silently. That was a bit much.

"Oh, geez," he said, getting up to stand in front of her. "I'm sorry."

"Ha!" she said, turning and stomping down the sidewalk. Dammit, she thought, he'd wanted to kiss Agatha! Not her, Autumn, but Agatha! She didn't want him to be attracted to Agatha. Autumn

Stanton wanted to feel his lips on hers, be held in those strong arms . . .

"Agatha, wait!" Graham called. He caught up with her and took her arm.

"Don't touch her—me!" she said, not looking at him. "I did nothing to warrant your advances, Mr. Kimble."

"I really do apologize," he said, pulling open the door to his office building.

"It occurs to me," she said, "that you were not as unaffected by Joyce St. James slithering all over you as you might have assumed. I was merely the recipient of your jangled libido."

"Wrong," he said, shaking his head. "I wanted to kiss you, Agatha."

"Don't say that!" she said, turning to face him, her eyes flashing. "You did not want to kiss Agatha Stanton!"

"Sure I did," he said, grinning at her. "In fact, I still do."

Autumn pursed her lips and said nothing more as they rode in the elevator to his floor. He slowly followed her down the hall to his office, humming off key. She impatiently tapped one clunky shoe on the floor as he unlocked the door. When he pushed it open, he stepped back with a dramatic sweep of his arm and another hundred-watt smile. She flounced into the office, sat down in her chair, and folded her arms across her chest.

Graham closed the door. "Do you find the prospect of my kissing you that distressing?" he said in a low voice.

Lord, no! she thought. Truth of the matter was, she was angry that Graham wasn't reacting to

Agatha the way she'd expected. And to top it off, she was jealous of Agatha. What did Agatha have that she didn't? Good grief, she was getting the crazies! She couldn't think straight!

"Agatha?"

"I don't know what to say, Graham," she said, slowly lifting her eyes to look at him. "I can honestly say that I'm terribly confused right now."

"That's my fault, because I rushed you. You're right, you know. I have lived in the fast lane. So, now I'm slowing down to step into your enchanting, old-fashioned world and do this properly. Miss Stanton." He extended his hand to her. "Would you do me the honor of allowing me to kiss you? Nothing wild, you understand, just a soft, sweet kiss. Please?" He waited anxiously for her response. Why it was suddenly so incredibly important, he didn't know, but he really needed to kiss this woman.

In almost detached fascination Autumn watched her trembling hand lift from her lap, then seem to float through the air toward Graham. His strong fingers closed around hers, and he gently pulled her up to stand in front of him.

He cradled her face in his hands, his gaze locked to hers, before he slowly, slowly lowered his head. Fleetingly, he brushed his lips over hers, then dropped his arms to gather her close to his chest as her hands crept up to circle his neck, her fingers inching into his thick hair.

His tongue slid over her bottom lip, seeking, then gaining entry to the sweetness within. Heat shimmered through her as she returned the kiss in total abandon. A shudder ripped through Graham, and the kiss intensified, and went on and on.

Yes! Graham's mind thundered.

Oh, yes! Autumn thought.

"Agatha," he gasped, tearing his mouth from hers.

"Who?" she said, taking an unsteady breath. Oh, darn it! Agatha was there again. "I—I . . ." she stammered, stepping back.

"As I said," Graham said hoarsely, "you're very special. You are also a very passionate, very desirable woman."

"But I'm not who you think I—"

"Don't feel guilty about our kiss," he interrupted. "It was wonderful. And it was ours. I'll get back to work now and leave you alone."

Autumn sank onto the edge of the desk as Graham walked toward his office.

"Graham?"

"Yes?" He stopped and turned toward her.

"I'm supposed to remind you to get a haircut."

"Thank you," he said, smiling at her. "For everything."

Three

Home had never looked so good.

With a grateful sigh, Autumn stepped into the shower and allowed the hot water to stream over her. When she was through she blow dried her hair into a tumble of strawberry-blond waves that fell to her shoulders. She dressed in black brushed-corduroy pants and a white cashmere sweater, and mascara, blush, and lip gloss erased the last traces of Agatha.

After dinner Autumn cleaned the kitchen, then wandered into her large living room and sank onto the sofa. She had the strange sensation that it had been ages since she'd been in her luxurious apartment. Had it only been that morning that she'd dressed as Agatha and gone blissfully off to Graham Kimble's office? Only a handful of hours had managed to turn her life upside down?

A large white cat strolled into the room. "Cricket," Autumn called. "Come here, sweetheart."

The cat was more interested in seeing what was being offered for dinner, and walked into the kitchen. Autumn sighed and thought of Graham and the kiss they had shared.

What a kiss it had been, she mused, pressing her fingertips to her lips. Desire, unexpectedly strong, had swept through her like a tidal wave, wreaking havoc with her sense of reality. There, in Graham's strong arms, she had experienced a kiss like none before. She could vividly recall the taste, feel, and aroma of him, and the memories sent a shiver through her once again.

But, dammit, he had kissed *Agatha*! He didn't even know Autumn, let alone find her attractive, pleasant, fun to be with. She wanted Graham to kiss *her*, hold *her*, tell *her* she had beautiful eyes. This was, without a doubt, the most ridiculous situation she had ever been in.

Was she behaving like a spoiled child? Autumn asked herself. She'd been the recipient of male attention since high school, when her braces had come off and her baby fat melted away, leaving lush curves and full breasts. She'd been raised in the world of the affluent but had been taught to work hard for her dreams. When her grandmother had died, she had received a large inheritance. She had invested the money wisely, but it had not deterred her from her goal of obtaining her doctoral degree. Except for her one disastrous affair with the dimwit who had resented the hours she'd spent studying, she'd had a carefree life.

Until now. Until Graham Kimble.

If she could chalk up her behavior as childish jealousy of Agatha, it would be easier to understand. Absurd, yet feasible. But it was more than that, and she knew it. Graham stirred something deep within her: a yearning, a heightened awareness of her femininity, a mixture of emotions that suspended her between wanting to laugh and cry. Something new and wondrous was happening to her because of Graham, and she wanted to go forward, discover more.

"But he doesn't even know me!" she cried aloud. She'd almost told him that Agatha was a fraud. After the kiss, she'd started to tell him, but he'd misinterpreted her blithering as Agatha's embarrassment over responding to his kiss. A half hour later a client had arrived, and Graham had left the office with the man to look at some property. Autumn had spent the afternoon alone. At five o'clock she'd locked the office and come home in a state of total depression.

She had to think this through. Graham was momentarily fascinated by Agatha, she decided. After all, Joyce St. James was an example of the type of woman he was undoubtedly used to. Agatha was different, refreshing, innocent, and all that jazz. The kiss could have been nothing more than an act of curiosity on his part to sample the wares of a less than worldly woman. That louse! That wasn't very nice! He could break poor little Agatha's heart.

But, she went on, he had probably satisfied his curiosity, and tomorrow he'd steer clear of Agatha. Then next week he could meet Autumn Stanton. She'd present herself honestly, openly, and leave the rest to fate. Well, she wasn't beyond nudging things along a bit with some feminine wiles. Nothing drastic, just careful attention to dress and makeup, a sincere interest in Graham and his career. Because she was very interested in Graham Kimble. Interested to the point that it was a tad frightening.

Again, Autumn pressed her fingers to her lips and recalled the kiss she'd shared with Graham, allowing the tingling sensations of desire to dance through her. His image floated before her eyes, his sun-streaked hair, and deep brown eyes, and beautiful smile. And his broad shoulders and long, muscular legs. He was the epitome of masculinity. And like never before, Autumn was so very aware that she was woman.

When she went to bed she fell asleep instantly, and dreamed of Graham.

Tuesday's outfit, if possible, was worse than Monday's. Autumn stood in front of the full-length mirror in her bedroom and wrinkled her nose at her reflection. The dress was yards and yards of mustard-yellow lightweight wool that hung in giant folds to midcalf. Her black oxfords were in place, her hair was parted off center and twisted into the lopsided bun. Her skin had a strange jaundiced cast to it.

"Poor Agatha," she said. "You look absolutely terrible! I hope Graham can stand the shock."

She planted a kiss on Cricket's head, grabbed her purse, and left the apartment with a bright smile on her face. Her depression of the previous night had dissipated. She had only a few more days to act out her charade, then Autumn could emerge. Graham would surely ignore Agatha as much as possible for the remainder of the week, and all would be well.

The office door was unlocked when Autumn arrived, and she peered in cautiously before entering. The aroma of coffee reached her as she stepped inside, and she saw that the brew had already been prepared. As she turned to her desk, she stopped dead in her tracks.

Right in the center of her desk was a bud vase with a single long-stemmed pink rose.

Her eyes wide, she moved forward, set her purse on the desk, and ran a fingertip over a velvet-soft petal.

"Like it?" a deep voice asked.

Autumn gasped and turned around. "Graham! You startled me." He was walking slowly toward her, wearing a dark blue suit, crisp white shirt, dark tie. The man just didn't quit! He was beautiful, absolutely beautiful! And he'd gotten a haircut. Wasn't that sweet?

"Do you like the rose?" he asked. Saints above, what was she wearing? It was worse than yesterday's monstrosity. She could smuggle an elephant under all that material. And the color? Good Lord.

"It's a lovely rose," she said. "But why is it here?"

"I wanted you to have it. I thought about you last night, Agatha," he said, his voice low.

Autumn sank onto her chair as her trembling legs refused to hold her. Graham had thought about Agatha? she wondered. He wasn't supposed to do that! And he had brought Agatha a rose?

Damn him! Was the man totally deranged? Blind as a bat? What was the matter with him?

"Don't be frightened of me, Agatha," he said, sitting on the edge of her desk. "There's nothing sinister about a man bringing a rose to the woman who shared his bed the night before."

"What?" she croaked.

"Relatively speaking," he added quickly. "I thought about you as I was trying to sleep. Thought about that kiss we shared. I had a very restless night. Alone. In that big bed. Thinking of you."

"Oh, dear heaven," she whispered, pressing her hands to her burning cheeks. She wished he'd get his tush off her desk! The material of his slacks was pulled tightly across his thigh, enticing her imagination. Did he sleep in pajamas or nude? Nude? That magnificent body naked? She was coming unglued!

"You're not sorry about the kiss, are you?" he asked, leaning slightly toward her.

"Well, I . . ."

"Morning, y'all," a voice boomed.

Autumn jumped, and Graham slid off the desk to greet the man who had entered the office.

"Bish!" he said. "I thought you were still in Denver."

"Flew in early this morning. Well, hello," he added, smiling at Autumn.

"Agatha Stanton, Bish Terzoni," Graham said.

"I can't tell you what a pleasure this is," Bish said, taking Autumn's hand and kissing the back of it.

"Stow it, Terzoni," Graham muttered.

"Excuse me," Autumn said, retrieving her hand as the phone began ringing. She reached for the receiver, acutely aware that Bish Terzoni's gaze was riveted on her. "It's Mr. Fisher," she said to Graham a moment later.

"I'll take it in my office. Mind your manners, Bish."

"Sure, Cracker. I don't gobble up secretaries so early in the morning."

"Hell," Graham said, striding into his office.

Bish wandered over to the coffeepot and poured himself a mug. Autumn observed him from beneath her lashes, deciding he was an extremely handsome and well-built man. He and Graham were obviously close friends and must have to step over swooning women when they entered a room.

"Coffee?" Bish asked pleasantly.

"I'll get it," she said, and stood and walked toward him. Why was he staring at her like that? she wondered. Oh, of course. She was wearing a supergross outfit, and he probably couldn't quite believe his eyes.

"Agatha," he said as she poured her coffee. "Interesting name. Very old-fashioned."

"I like it," she said, returning to her desk and sitting down.

A rumble of laughter escaped from Bish's throat, causing Autumn to look up at him and frown. A wide grin on his face, he shook his head, then sat down in the chair in front of her desk. He propped one ankle over the other knee and smiled at her.

"Okay, Autumn," he said, "what's the con? What in the hell are you up to?"

She opened her mouth, but no sound came out. A rushing noise echoed in her ears.

"I beg your pardon?" she finally managed to say.

"It's a great disguise, but I've seen too many pictures of you not to recognize you."

"Pictures of me? Me?"

"In the den of your parents' home in Pacific Heights. Your father is a long-time client of mine. I own an investment firm. I had a postcard from him the other day saying France was terrific. The jig is up, Autumn Stanton. I know exactly who you are."

"Damn," she said, her shoulders slumping. "Of all the rotten luck. Now, I suppose, you can hardly wait to spill the beans to your buddy Cracker. That's a dumb thing to call him, by the way."

"Cracker and I go way back to our boyhood days. So? What's the deal, Autumn? I'm a fair man. At least let me hear your side of this fiasco."

"Mr. Terzoni—"

"It's Bish."

"Bish, look, I'm not playing some weird game here. I'm conducting some research for my doctoral thesis in psychology. My theory is that women reap what they sow in today's society. Agatha represents an unworldly, innocent woman, who evokes respect in men because of her image."

"She's something all right," Bish said, chuckling. "That's the freakiest dress I've ever seen."

"Great, huh?" Autumn said, smiling. "Bish, please don't tell Graham who I am. I realize he's your friend, but I need this data. It's only for the rest of the week. Then I'll be Autumn until Aunt Nancy gets back."

"Nancy is your aunt? Never mind. Autumn, this

is a lot more complicated than you realize. Cracker has this crazy notion in his head . . . No, it's not my place to discuss that. Damn, this could turn into a helluva mess."

"Why? I'm here, then I'll disappear."

"Tell me this, Autumn. Has Graham behaved the way you assumed he would when confronted with Agatha?"

"Well, not exactly, no. But I think I've figured that out."

"Oh?"

"He's intrigued by Agatha. Curious. He has been more attentive than I ever dreamed he'd be, but his interest will lag any minute now."

"Don't count on it," Bish said into his mug.

"Pardon?"

"Nothing. Autumn, I'm caught in the middle here. I don't want to see anyone get hurt."

"No one will! Agatha will no longer exist by next week."

"Are you planning on telling Cracker the whole story when you change back into Autumn?"

"I hadn't thought that far ahead."

"Then that's my deal. I'll keep my mouth shut on the condition that you tell him the truth when Agatha croaks. Damn. I have a feeling I'm making a terrible mistake. A lot can happen in a few days."

"You're overreacting, Bish. I agree to your terms. I'll explain it all to Graham when I become Autumn. I promise."

"I hope I'm not sorry I—"

"Fisher sure does get long-winded," Graham said, coming out of his office. "So, did you two get acquainted?"

"Yep," Bish said. "I feel as though I've known Agatha for a very long time. Got a spare minute, Cracker? I want to double-check a couple things on those condo plans."

"You bet. Come on in. Your stuff is on my board."

Autumn watched as the two men disappeared into Graham's office, then sank back in her chair. A few million people lived in San Francisco and she had to bump into a friend of her father's! Well, she'd bought the time she needed from Bish Terzoni. What was he so anxious about in the first place? Surely he realized that Agatha wasn't Graham's type. Bish had insinuated that someone could get hurt, but the only vulnerable person in the scenario was sweet, innocent Agatha, and her days were numbered. And while she, Autumn, was admittedly slightly whacky since meeting Graham Kimble, there was certainly no risk of his breaking her heart. She simply wanted an opportunity to explore further the new sensations he was creating within her without Agatha in the way. Bish Terzoni was an Italian worry-wart! Now, if she could just get Graham to quit doing dorky things like bringing a rose to Agatha, everything would be fine.

"Well?" Graham asked Bish. "No, wait." He closed the door. "What do you think of Agatha?"

"She's . . . um, something. Very unusual."

"I realize she dresses off the wall, but I can get used to that. I hope."

"Dammit, Cracker, this whole scheme of yours is crazy! You don't even know Agatha. You're acting like you've already made up your mind to marry her!"

"Listen to me, Bish. Something is happening here, and I'm not imagining it. Agatha is special, rare, one in a million. She makes me feel fantastic because I could protect her, keep her from harm."

Bish groaned and stared up at the ceiling.

"I couldn't get her off my mind last night. I couldn't sleep because I kept replaying that kiss in my mind—"

"You kissed her?" Bish roared.

"Shh! She's very sensitive. But yes, I kissed her, and I'm telling you, she is passion waiting to break loose. She's everything I want in a woman."

"Give me a break, Kimble. Next you'll be saying you're in love with her."

"No, love is some romantic's gimmick for selling candy on Valentine's Day. I'm not kidding myself about that stuff. But everything else is there in Agatha. She's intelligent, she wants a career, but won't put it ahead of her family. I couldn't believe it when I found myself thinking about her last night. I was really eager to see her this morning."

"You could see her in a crowd in that dress," Bish grumbled.

"No one is perfect, Terzoni."

"Cracker, don't do this, I beg of you. Call Champagne. Find out what she wanted to do with that chicken soup. Forget Agatha Stanton!"

"No!"

"Women are not always what they present themselves to be, Cracker. Didn't you learn anything from what happened to me five years ago? Sweet little Gina, who I married because she told me she was pregnant. Then two weeks later she disappeared, and the next thing I saw was an affidavit saying she had had a miscarriage, along with divorce papers demanding a hunk of money. Gina was a phony from the word go. I'd been dating her for months and didn't realize it. You just met Agatha, Graham. You don't know a damn thing about her!"

"Yes, I do."

"I should have stayed in Denver. This is a nightmare. Look, will you at least take it slow? Hey, how's this? I'll fly you down to Malibu to see your folks for a few days, like, say, the rest of the week. Then, next Monday you view this whole thing fresh."

"Nope."

"Dammit to hell!"

"Why are you so strung out? I thought you'd be happy for me, Bish."

"Oh, Cracker, I don't know what to say. I don't want to see you get hurt."

"Agatha isn't Gina, Bish. You judge women too harshly because of what you went through. I know how much you wanted that baby, and you got nothing out of the deal but an empty wallet. You're not being fair to Agatha. Give her a chance, okay?"

"Yeah. A deal is a deal."

"What?"

"Nothing. Well, I've said all I can. I'll be around, Cracker, if you need to glue the pieces back together."

"You worry too much. Come on. Take a look at these fantastic plans I've drawn up for you. You've got a genius for a best friend, old buddy."

"I think your old buddy is on the verge of an ulcer!"

While Graham and Bish were holed up in the other office, Autumn alternated between processing the mail and sticking her nose in the beautiful pink rose. It smelled heavenly, and she smiled each time she inhaled the delicate fragrance. But with each sniff and smile came a frown as she recalled what Graham had been saying before Bish arrived.

Graham had thought of her last night? She repeated in her mind over and over. Thought of her while he was in bed? He had spent a restless night as he'd recalled the kiss they'd shared? Oh, this was terrible. It couldn't be possible. Graham Kimble couldn't be infatuated with Agatha Stanton! But there sat the rose as tangible evidence that his thoughts had focused on Agatha on his way to work that morning.

"Oh, dear," she murmured. "What am I going to do?"

"Something, and fast!" Bish said, striding toward her desk.

"What?"

"Make sure Agatha does something, anything, to turn Graham off! Listen to me, Autumn. Graham is captivated by Agatha. He thinks she's a sweet, innocent, old-fashioned girl, just what he's been looking for. This has to stop before he gets hurt."

"I never intended for him— Oh, no! Agatha will have to be called out of town right away."

"No! Cracker would just wait for her to get back.

He has to decide on his own that Agatha isn't the one for him. I don't know how you're going to do it, but do it!"

"But—"

"All set," Graham said, coming out of his office.

"Good," Bish said, nodding. "Well, I'll let you get back to work. It was interesting meeting you, Agatha."

"Yes, interesting," she said, smiling weakly.

"See ya, Bish," Graham said. "Don't worry about a thing."

"Hell," Bish said. He was frowning as he left the office and slammed the door behind him.

"Italians are very volatile," Graham said, grinning. "I could use another cup of coffee."

Autumn watched as he walked to the coffeepot, her gaze sweeping over his perfect physique. He was magnificent. And he was interested in another woman. Agatha.

Autumn sighed. A wobbly sigh. A sad sigh. A sigh that brought tears prickling at the back of her eyes. She'd been sniffing a rose that belonged to someone else, had savored a kiss that hadn't been hers, was basking in the attention of a man who didn't even know she existed! She wanted to strangle Agatha Stanton! She dug in her purse for a tissue and discreetly blew her nose.

"Agatha?" Graham said. turning toward her.

"I suppose," she said miserably.

"What's wrong?"

"Nothing. I've just got a slight cold. I've been fighting it for the past week." That, at least, was the truth.

"I have to drive out and look at Fisher's property.

I'd like you to come along and take notes. It'll be a nice outing. I'll need about a half hour to get organized."

"Fine."

"Are you sure you're all right?"

"Yes, of course. I'll be ready to go whenever you say."

"Great." He smiled at her, then went into his office.

"Wonderful," she muttered.

She leaned back in her chair and tapped the erasure end of a pencil against her chin. Things were getting out of control, but the situation wasn't hopeless. Bish was right. Graham had to figure out on his own that Agatha was a poor choice for him. The fact that he was attracted to her at all was difficult to fathom, but to each his own. Agatha had to be seen as the dud she was, or Autumn would never stand a chance with Graham Kimble.

Not only that, Autumn mused, but feelings were involved. Graham could very well get hurt if Agatha disappeared while he was still interested in her. Autumn had assured Aunt Nancy that Graham would suffer no ill effects from her plan. She had to get things back on track! There was suddenly a great deal at stake: Graham's emotional happiness, the promise to Aunt Nancy, the fact that Autumn had never intentionally hurt anyone in her life, *and* that she wanted Graham to view *her* as a woman.

"My life is in the blender," Autumn muttered. "Some psychologist I am!"

Shaking her head, she picked up the pile of work

Graham had dropped on her desk and began sorting through it. She was busy filing when he emerged from his office.

"Ready to go?" he asked.

"Yes, certainly," she said. She stuffed a notebook and pencil in her purse, then flicked on the answering machine.

Clouds were rolling across the sky as Autumn and Graham left the underground garage in his bronze Ferrari. Autumn had made no comment about the sleek automobile but had silently praised it. Oh, how she'd love to be behind the wheel of this fantastic car, feeling all that power beneath her hands. Agatha, however, was totally unimpressed.

Graham commanded the Ferrari with expertise. Autumn watched him from beneath her lashes, his large, strong hands gripping the wheel with confidence; the muscles of his thighs flexing seductively as he pressed the pedals. Tingling desire feathered up her spine, and she forced herself to look out the side window.

"We're going across the Golden Gate to Marin County," Graham said. "Fisher has a piece of property up there. He wants a weekend home built, and wants it to blend into the environment."

"Do you agree with him?"

"Absolutely. Don't you?"

"A house is a house," she said, shrugging. Brother! she thought. The members of the environmentalist group she belonged to would toss her out on her ear if they heard that! "I'd build what I wanted whether it jarred the scenery or not."

"Oh," Graham said, frowning slightly.

"My cousin Autumn and I get into some heated arguments about that sort of thing," she went on. "She's always signing petitions, picketing, the whole bit, to preserve the environment."

"I've signed a petition or two myself," he said.

"Autumn would adore you," she said, smiling sweetly.

"I'll view it as a tremendous challenge to change your views on this," he said. "We'll have some great debates. It'll be . . . very stimulating."

Oh, terrific! Autumn thought.

"Your friend Bish is a very handsome man," she said, watching Graham closely for his reaction.

He chuckled. "That's no news flash," he said. "Women tell me that all the time. Terzoni has more women than he can handle. Bish and I operate on the principle of honesty in our relationships. We don't make promises we don't intend to keep. Everything is upfront. I have very strong convictions about honesty."

Autumn rolled her eyes.

"Here's the Golden Gate Bridge," Graham said. "Just look at it. You'd think I'd be used to it by now, but it awes me every time I drive across it."

"It was designed by Joseph Baermann Strauss," Autumn said. "Everyone thought he was slightly crazy, and it took him years to convince people to build the bridge. Do you know that during the first four years of construction, not one man was killed due to Strauss's elaborate safety precautions? He spent eighty thousand dollars on a net, which nineteen men fell into and lived to tell about. They formed the 'Halfway to Hell' club."

"Fascinating," Graham said.

"It really is. The bridge opened on May twenty-seventh, 1937, and two hundred and two thousand people walked across it. Then— Oh, sorry. I'm getting rather carried away."

"And I'm enjoying every minute," he said seriously. "You're a remarkable woman, Agatha. There's so much about you I want to discover. I'm very grateful to Nancy for bringing you into my life."

Oh, no! Autumn sighed silently. She couldn't go on with this charade. It was getting worse by the minute. She was going to tell him the truth and hope for the best. Surely he'd see the humor in all of this . . . wouldn't he? She'd transform herself into Autumn, and they would go from there. Wouldn't they? Well, she'd have to take her chances and tell him the truth. But not in the middle of a bridge almost two hundred and fifty feet above water. Stupid, she was not!

Graham hummed quietly as they drove, giving every indication that he was relaxed and thoroughly enjoying the outing. Autumn was a nervous wreck. After passing through Sausalito, he consulted a hand-drawn map, then turned off the main thoroughfare. A half hour later he slowed to weave the Ferrari over narrow back roads. Finally, shaking his head, he stopped the car.

"Fisher said his land was in a nice, natural area," he said, "and he wasn't kidding. My car is too low to take these ruts in the road. As far as I can tell, we're about a mile away. Are you game?"

"Oh, yes! It's beautiful here," Autumn said. And quiet and isolated, and if Graham murdered her when she told him the truth about Agatha, they'd never find her body! Oh, for Pete's sake, she was getting crazy.

"That's my girl," he said. "Let's go."

The area was heavily wooded, and the sounds of singing birds and chattering squirrels filled the air. The sun peeked from behind the clouds and sent a warming glow skittering through the leaves of the trees.

"It's hard to believe we were just in a crowded city," Graham said. "It's so peaceful here. A person could really get in touch with himself, make sure he's keeping himself on track."

"And being honest," Autumn said, and swallowed heavily. "Graham, there's something I—"

"Agatha," he interrupted, cradling her face in his hands. "I'm going to kiss you. Here, in this beautiful woods. Right now. Okay?"

She couldn't speak past the lump in her throat and simply nodded as she gazed up into his warm brown eyes.

As though she were made of the most delicate china, he gathered her into his arms, nestling her against his hard chest as his mouth covered hers. She moaned softly. Her eyes drifted closed and her hands lifted to his neck. Their tongues met, and their desires instantly soared.

Autumn's body hummed with the sensual joy of receiving Graham's masculine power. Her breasts ached and her nipples grew taut as a fiery heat began deep within her.

She wanted this man to make love to her, to fill her, consume her. She wanted him not only to quell the flame of passion within her, but to possess her mind, heart, and soul as well.

Inch by emotional inch, Autumn Stanton was falling in love with Graham Kimble.

Four

Graham seemed to lose touch with reality as he immersed himself in the sweetness of Agatha's kiss. The blood pounded in his veins, and his manhood swelled to an aching hardness. His hands roamed over her back, feeling nothing more than the bulky material of her dress.

But his imagination went further. He saw himself drawing the dress away from her to discover the mysteries beneath. He saw his hands on her pale skin, his mouth seeking her breasts. Every inch of her would be disclosed to him as she lay naked beneath him, eager to receive him into the honeyed warmth of her femininity. He would bring her to a fever pitch of passion, shattering her inhibitions and old-fashioned standards, until she was writhing with desire and begging him to come to her.

A whispering voice penetrated Graham's hazy mind, increasing its volume until the message roared in his head. Sex. His resolve to view this woman as an intelligent human being with goals and values matching his had been overridden by the driving needs of his body.

What he had viewed for so long as the natural order of things, as a pleasurable, satisfying inter-lude between himself and a willing woman, now brought a wave of disgust. He had not, after all, been accepting of Agatha's outward appearance but had been waiting for the moment when he could strip away the disturbing trimmings and gain access to the woman beneath. He was Gra-ham Kimble, fast-lane hustler, and it caused a knot to twist painfully in his gut.

He tore his mouth from hers and stepped back. "No!" he said. "Dammit, no!"

Autumn swayed on her feet, drawing an unsteady breath as she looked up at him in confusion.

"Graham?" she whispered, her voice husky with passion.

He turned his back to her, taking deep breaths as he stared at the sky, striving for control. His shoulders were rigid, and the tension emanating from his taut body seemed to strike Autumn with the force of a physical blow.

He was rejecting her. she thought frantically. She had returned his kiss with an abandon she had never known before, and he was rejecting her! Her desire for Graham had felt so right, as though she had traveled far to find the haven within his arms.

"I'm sorry," he said, turning slowly to face her. "I never intended to get so carried away."

"You didn't! *We* didn't. We shared that kiss, Graham. You didn't force yourself on me."

"You don't understand, Agatha," he said, raking his hand through his hair. "I wanted more. I wanted to make love to you. I would have taken you right there on that grass under those trees. I realize that probably shocks and frightens you, but it's the truth."

"It doesn't frighten me," she said, relief sweeping through her. "I wanted you, too."

"Don't say that! This is all my fault. I know you don't have casual sex."

"Well, no, of course not, but—"

"I'm from the fast lane, remember? Everyone understands how the game's played. I take what's offered to me, and no one gets hurt. But you would, don't you see? You'd feel betrayed. I've never met anyone like you before, Agatha, and I'm beginning to realize I don't deserve to be in your world. All I could think about was taking off your clothes and making love to you!"

Really? Autumn thought. Graham wanted her that much? Heaven knew how much she wanted him, and it wouldn't have come remotely close to being casual sex. She was a breath away from falling deeply in love with this man. And it was wonderful.

"Agatha." He moved closer to her and placed his hands on her shoulders. "Listen to me. I told you that you're special, and you are. Rare, and special, and lovely. You present yourself so openly, without fancy makeup and glamorous clothes. I'm so sick

of flashy women, who attract men with their outward appearance. Don't ever change, Agatha. Stay
exactly who you are. But be patient with me, okay?
I've got a lot to learn about being with someone like
you."

Don't ever change? she repeated silently, incredulously. He didn't want her to wear makeup or
pretty clothes? No eye shadow to enhance her
green eyes, no sexy high heels to show off her legs?
He was sick of women who made the most of their
appearance? But Autumn did! Oh, dear heaven,
what was she going to do?

"Don't frown," he said, kissing her quickly on
the forehead. "Come on, let's go for a hike. We'll follow this road and it should lead us right to Fisher's
property."

"Yes, fine," she said absently. "I'll just get my
purse out of the car."

They started down the narrow, bumpy path, and
Autumn's oxfords almost immediately felt like
heavy, uncomfortable bricks. She went over and
over in her mind everything Graham had said.

He was definitely enthralled with Agatha. If she
told him that Agatha didn't really exist and was in
actuality Autumn, who enjoyed wearing attractive,
fashionable clothes, knew how to use makeup to
her full benefit, all would be lost. She never dressed
gaudily, but she was sure that to Graham, anything more than Agatha's drab exterior would
shout flash and dash, a woman from the fast lane.

But how long would Graham's infatuation with
Agatha last? Autumn wondered as she tromped
along. He was in a phase. This had to be a passing

fancy, a momentary sense of boredom with his life that he would laugh about later.

For now, she decided, she would have to remain as Agatha. The deception was risky, but to disclose herself as Autumn while Graham was such a space case was guaranteed disaster. She had no choice but to wait and watch for the proper moment to tell him the truth.

"Look at those squirrels," Graham said. "Aren't they great?"

"They probably have fleas," she muttered. Smooth move, she thought smugly. What Graham liked, she wouldn't. Agatha was going to outdo herself as a disagreeable dud.

"Probably," he said, chuckling, "but they're still cute. Smart little buggers, too, the way they store up food for the winter. The original bankers with savings accounts."

She laughed in spite of herself. Oh, this man was so dear, and warm, and wonderful. Was this how love happened, she wondered, with a rush of emotions that warmed one within like rich brandy? At that moment there was nowhere else she wished to be than here, hiking through the woods with Graham, her feet aching and the taste of his kiss lingering on her lips.

"How are you doing?" he asked as he pulled his tie loose and stuffed it into his pocket. "We would have worn different clothes if I'd known we were going to take on this trek."

"I'm all right," she said. "I'm not really into physical fitness, though. Now, my cousin Autumn would be right in her element. She jogs, swims, plays tennis."

"Well, you have your studies to be concerned with."

"So does she," Autumn rushed on. "Autumn and I are in the same doctorate program. My cousin is a very intelligent woman. I admire her self-discipline. She's constantly sought after by men, but she's determined to get her degree." Goodness, she mused, self-sell was embarrassing! If only Graham would show a flicker of interest in Autumn. Raise an eyebrow in curiosity, or say, "Oh?" in a way that indicated he'd like to hear more about Autumn.

"Oh?" Graham said.

Hooray! she mentally cheered.

"Maybe we should introduce Autumn to Bish," he went on. "I'm sure he'd enjoy going out with a woman with brains for a change."

Dammit, she cursed silently. Nothing was working! "Maybe," she mumbled.

"Do you see Autumn often?"

"Every day. We share an apartment." And a body, for crying out loud! "Uh-oh. Look at those clouds."

He glanced at the darkening sky. "We'd better get this done as quickly as possible, before that storm breaks. We're looking for— There it is. That big white rock marks the edge of Fisher's property. Let's walk off the road and see what he has."

The plot of land was dense with trees, and as storm clouds continued to gather, an eerie darkness fell. Graham rattled off information which Autumn quickly scribbled in her notebook, keeping one eye on the sky. She was impressed with the ideas that flowed off the top of Graham's head and how much importance he placed on conserving as many of the beautiful trees as possible. An A-frame structure, he said, would provide maximum space without requiring major destruction of the natural environment.

"That should do it for now," he said finally. "I'll hash all this over with Fisher and see what he thinks."

"It sounds fantastic! I'm sure he'll be pleased with— Oh! I felt a drop of rain!"

"Let's get out of here!"

She stuffed the notebook into her purse, then Graham grabbed her hand and they started back toward the road. They had just reached it when the heavens opened.

"Oh, Lord!" Autumn shrieked as the rain poured over them, drenching them in an instant.

"Damn," Graham said, and hurried her along the road.

The cold rain fell in torrents, making visibility difficult and transforming the dirt road into a sea of mud. Autumn's wool dress soaked up the water, becoming heavier and heavier. Her shoes sank deeper into the muddy puddles, making a noise like a suction cup each time she pulled them free.

For some reason that she couldn't fathom, after a few minutes she found the whole predicament hysterically funny. She had a vision of herself sinking to the center of the earth if Graham let go of her hand. It was all so absurd, and she burst into laughter.

"Agatha?" Graham said, coming to a complete stop. "Don't panic, okay? We're not in danger, we're just wet. I'll get you out of here, I promise."

She tried to speak but only managed to laugh

even louder. She wrapped her arms around her stomach and whooped with merriment.

Graham frowned. "Why are you laughing?"

"It's . . ." She gasped for breath. "It's just so-o-o funny. This dress has got to weigh twenty pounds! My shoes are sticking like glue and . . . I don't think I can go another step!" She dissolved into laughter again.

He appeared totally confused as he stared at her, then a smile tugged at his lips, broadening into a wide grin.

"You are really something," he said. "You constantly surprise me. Look, there's no lightning so we'll be safe under the trees. It might be a little drier."

"Lead on, Macduff," she said, smiling brightly. "Providing, of course, I can move!"

He led her back off the road to a thick grouping of trees. The branches and leaves provided an umbrella, and the grass was nearly dry. They sank to the ground and leaned back against a wide trunk. Autumn pulled the few remaining pins from her hair, then drew her fingers through the wet tresses.

"I wondered how long your hair was," Graham said. "I bet it's very pretty when it's dry, and free like that. Never mind. It's nice in the bun, too." Don't do it, Kimble! he told himself. Don't try to change her. He had to accept Agatha as she was. Unless . . .

His thoughts skidded to an abrupt halt as he stared at her. She fluffed her hair with her fingers, then lifted a wad of her dress and wrung out the water.

Maybe, he mused, Agatha was protecting herself with her outward appearance, using it as a shield against men. She had spoken of a lover who had not been tolerant of her need to spend hours studying. Had she been so badly hurt that she had withdrawn behind a wall?

He had to think this through. To give Agatha any hint that he wished she were more attractive would destroy her and what they were building together. But it would be cruel not to help her gain self-esteem, show her she had nothing to fear by combining her beauty with her brains. Still, it was risky. If he did convince her to emerge from her cocoon, he might lose her to another man. As it was, the guys he knew wouldn't give her a second glance the way she looked now. He cared for her, he really did. She was everything he wanted in a wife and the mother of his children. He'd buy her a big house and tuck her away to tend to their family.

What a crummy, selfish thing to do, he told himself the next instant. He was a real louse. He should lead Agatha gently from behind her protective wall to a place of sunshine and warmth, where she could be everything she was meant to be. He should, but would he? What if he lost her?

"Brrr," she said. "I'm freezing."

"What?" he asked. "Yeah, it's chilly. I'd give you my jacket, but it's soaking wet. The rain has let up a little. I think we should go back to the car, and I can turn on the heater. I just hope I can drive out in that mud."

"Okay," she said, struggling to get up.

He helped her to her feet, then circled her shoulders with his arm and pulled her close. Autumn smiled in contentment as they walked along, relishing the strength and warmth of his body.

At last they reached the car, and Graham hurried to open the door for her. Autumn hesitated, peering down at her soggy dress, then at the plush interior of the Ferrari.

"I can't get in there," she said. "I'll ruin the upholstery. The rain has stopped, so why don't we stand here and dry out for a while?"

"You'll catch pneumonia. I don't care about the car. Get in, Agatha."

"Don't you have a blanket or something?"

"Of course," he said, snapping his fingers. "What a dope. I have a blanket in the trunk."

He retrieved the blanket and began to spread it over the seat.

"That isn't going to work, Graham," she said.

"Why not?"

"This thing I'm wearing is actually dripping. I'll soak right through that blanket and ruin the upholstery."

"I don't care! Get in the car!"

"Nope," she said, shaking her head. "The only solution is for me to take off my dress."

"What?" he exclaimed. "Do what?"

"Then I'll wrap up in the blanket. May I have it, please?"

"I don't know about this, Agatha," he said, pulling the blanket from the car. "Are you sure you want to strip, I mean, disrobe in a public place?"

"You're the only one here, Graham. Would you please turn your back so I may commence? I really am very cold."

"You bet," he said, spinning around. She was

taking off her dress! he thought. He couldn't handle this. He was a sinner, not a saint. He wanted to see the true Agatha. No! He was thinking like a sleazeball again. She trusted him enough to take her dress off, and he wouldn't betray that trust. But, oh, he was dying!

"There," she said. "All set."

He drew a steadying breath and turned slowly to face her. She was covered from chin to bare toes with the blanket, and he swore silently as he realized he was disappointed that he wasn't going to get even the slightest glimpse of her body.

"Cute toes," he muttered, and scooped up her wet things and tossed them into the trunk.

Autumn laughed softly and slid onto the seat, snuggling deeper into the cozy blanket. Her bra, panties, and full-length silk slip were damp, but she was definitely more comfortable. Agatha, she supposed, had acted out of character by removing the dress, but that was just too darn bad. Autumn had some rights, too, and turning into a human icicle was not high on her list of fun things to do!

Graham concentrated on maneuvering the Ferrari over the muddy road. He told himself that his entire attention was needed to accomplish the task.

He told himself it didn't matter that Agatha was next to him wrapped in a blanket, minus her dress. Then he told himself he was lying through his teeth.

"You're supposed to pick up your shirts at the laundry today," she said pleasantly. "Tomorrow you're to call to make an appointment to have your car serviced."

"Thanks," he said gruffly.

"The mechanic won't find anything wrong with the heater. It's working like a charm. My hair is dry already."

He glanced at her, then did a double take when he saw the shiny, wavy strawberry-blond hair that tumbled in disarray to her shoulders.

Good Lord! he thought, forcing his attention back to the road. Her hair was incredible! Oh, to sink his hands into it, bury his face in its silken beauty, inhale its fragrance. Should he tell her how lovely it was flowing free instead of pulled into that grim bun? Damn, every man who saw that hair would fantasize, just as he was doing now. No, he wasn't going to say a word.

"Your hair is very lovely like that," he said. What? Oh, hell! "Do you think you might consider wearing it loose? It's extremely becoming."

"Why, thank you, Graham," she said. "Autumn wears her hair like this, but . . . Yes, I think I might try it. Heaven knows that Autumn gets oodles of compliments on her hair."

"Wonderful," he said dismally.

She smiled and pulled the blanket more securely around her. It was a soft, fluffy wool and felt heavenly against her skin. She allowed her imagination to paint delightful pictures of herself being caressed by Graham instead of the blanket, of his naked body gleaming in the moonlight, or candlelight, or the glow from a fireplace. There they would be, Autumn and Graham . . . and Agatha.

"Oh, pooh!" Autumn said.

And then she sneezed.

It wasn't a quiet little ladylike sneeze, but a loud, drawn-out, two-syllable "Aaa-*choo!*"

Graham jerked his head around in surprise. "You're sick!" he yelled.

She jumped. "You don't have to holler," she said. "You scared me to death! All I did was sneeze."

"Sneeze! You practically blew the windshield out!"

"Why are you yelling?"

"Because it's all my fault, dammit! You told me you had a cold, and I took you out to the middle of nowhere, then got you drenched to the skin so you had to strip down to your bare bottom!"

"I certainly did no such thing!"

"You took your damn tent off, didn't you? And now you're sick!"

"I—aaa-*choo!*"

"Dammit!"

"Would you kindly quit swearing and screaming your head off?" she said. "I may have a tiny case of the sniffles, but it's nothing to throw a fit about. What do you do if someone gets the flu? Shoot them? Whatever is your problem, Graham?" Then she sneezed three times in rapid succession.

"Oh, Lord!" he said, rolling his eyes. "Some protector I am. You're sick, Agatha. Sick, do you hear me?"

"All of Marin County can hear you. Oh-h-h, my head."

"What's wrong with it? Talk to me."

"It hurts! My head hurts, my throat hurts, my nose hurts, and my teeth hurt! There! Are you satisfied? I'll probably be dead by midnight, having sneezed myself into oblivion."

"Don't say that!"

"I was kidding! All I need is a couple of aspirin and some juice, and I'll be fine."

"Where do you live? I'm taking you home."

"Don't be silly. I left my car at your office building."

"Listen up, Agatha Stanton. If you think I'm letting you drive around San Francisco wrapped in a blanket and sick as a dog, you're nuts! Where do you live?"

Autumn frowned, sneezed, then frowned again. She really did feel awful, she thought. All she wanted to do was crawl into bed and sleep. A drummer was beating steadily in her head, and her throat was on fire. So, fine, Graham could take her home. Her apartment was beautifully decorated and she'd done it all herself, but she'd simply say the style and flair had been genius Autumn at work, which was the truth.

"Well?" he said.

She rattled off her address, then leaned her head back and closed her eyes.

"That's only a few blocks from my place," he said. "Oh, Agatha, I'm so sorry you don't feel well. I should have checked the weather before we went out there. Will Autumn be around to look after you?"

"Autumn? No, she's unavailable at the moment."

"Don't worry." He patted her knee. "I'll stay with you."

"Fine," she mumbled. He'd what? she asked herself foggily. Oh, who cared? She just wanted to go to sleep for five years.

The trip back across the Golden Gate Bridge was

comprised of a sleepy Autumn sneezing and sniffling, and a crabby Graham swearing. At Autumn's apartment building, he parked in the visitors section, then assisted her out of the car.

"Eight fourteen," she said when he asked her apartment number. "That's on the eighth floor."

"Yes, I know," he said, and tucked her close to his side as they entered the building.

In the elevator she leaned her head on his chest and closed her eyes again. He tipped his head forward and inhaled the fresh scent of her hair, lifting one hand to sift his fingers through the silky strands.

Lovely, he thought, but then he had known it would be. Damn, it really was his fault that she was so sick. Taking her to Fisher's property had been off the wall in the first place. He'd never asked Nancy to go to job sites with him, as he was perfectly capable of jotting down his own notes. But he'd wanted to be with Agatha and had hauled her out there with no regard for her well-being. He'd certainly found out a great deal about himself since he'd met Agatha Stanton. And none of it would earn him a Boy Scout badge.

When they entered her apartment, he looked around in surprise. The living room and dining room were decorated in warm earth tones, a skillful blending of rusts and browns and deep greens, with touches of white to lighten the effect.

"This is some place," he said. "It's warm, but has class. It's really a sharp apartment."

"Autumn decorated it. She has marvelous taste and imagination. She started with a bare room and transformed it into this palace of splendor. That woman is unbelievable, just incredible!"

"Good for her," he said. "Let's get you into bed."

"Aaa-*choo!*"

"Now!"

Autumn's bedroom was done in delicate shades of mint green and yellow, with daisies on the spread covering the queen-size bed. Graham pulled back the blankets and fluffed the pillow.

"Where's your nightgown?" he asked.

"Hanging behind the bathroom door," she said, sinking onto the bed. Uh-oh, she thought an instant later as Graham headed across the room to the bathroom.

"I'll be damned," he said, and she cringed. He returned carrying a powder-blue satin nightgown with thin straps and a low-cut bodice. "This is yours?" he asked, holding it out in front of him for a better look.

"Autumn gave it to me. I prefer flannel jammies myself. With bunnies on them. Or kittens. Kittens are nice. Oh, hello, Cricket," she said as the cat wandered into the room. "Graham, this is Cricket, my cat."

"Hello." he said absently, still staring at the nightgown.

"May I have my nightgown, please?"

"What? Oh, sure, here. You change and get into bed. I'll go fix you some juice."

Autumn's head was buzzing by the time she'd slipped her underclothes off and her nightgown on. With a grateful sigh she slipped between the blankets and closed her eyes. The fact that Graham Kimble was wandering around her apartment was unimportant. All she wanted to do was sleep.

A few minutes later, Graham peered into the bedroom to be certain Agatha was in bed. His breath caught in his throat and the blood pounded in his veins when he saw her. His gaze swept over her, and he swallowed heavily.

She was lying on her back, the blankets pulled up to her waist. Her full, tempting breasts were barely covered by the satin nightgown. Her ivory skin looked like velvet and beckoned to him to touch and kiss her. Her hair, blond, gold, and red, was spread on the pillow in an enchanting disarray.

His manhood stirred, his heart raced, his breathing quickened. She was beautiful. She was everything and more than he had imagined might be hidden beneath the unattractive exterior she chose for herself. He wanted this woman with a passion he'd never felt before. He would protect her, cherish her, make her always smile and never cry.

"I'll be damned," he whispered. "I'm in love with Agatha." But he didn't believe in love. Or hadn't until now, until Agatha Stanton. It had hit him like a ton of bricks, and he knew it was true. He loved her.

So, now what? he wondered, sinking onto a chair and staring at her. He was back to square one. Agatha deserved the chance to discover her beauty, explore her femininity. At his suggestion she had already agreed to wear her hair loose. With gentle guidance he could take her farther, step by step, to her full potential of loveliness.

But when she emerged from her cocoon as the glorious butterfly, would she realize how much she had missed and want to make up for lost time? Would she pat him on the head, thank him for his trouble, and walk out of his world? Dammit, he'd just found her and didn't want to lose her! He loved her, was in love for the first time, and Agatha was his!

If he kept his mouth shut, she'd stay as she was. She'd wear her unsightly clothes and ugly shoes, and go unnoticed by the lusting men of San Francisco. They'd brush past her to get to the Betty Bazooms, and Agatha would concentrate only on him. Rotten. He was being totally rotten again. Selfish, and wrong, and rotten.

"Damn," he muttered. He loved Agatha, and because he did he owed it to her to allow her to make choices for herself. He had to show her what she could have, who she could be, then leave her alone to decide what she wanted to do. Because he loved her, he would have to risk losing her.

He pushed himself to his feet and stood beside the bed for a long moment. Then he walked into the living room, found paper and a pen on the desk, and wrote a note saying there was no juice or soup in the kitchen. He would go home to change, buy some groceries, and return as quickly as possible.

After propping the note on the nightstand, he brushed his lips lightly over Agatha's, then left the apartment, taking her keys with him.

He was in love, he thought as he drove away, and had never been so depressed in his entire life!

Five

Autumn stirred but did not open her eyes. She
reached out her hand to find Cricket and stroked
the cat's soft, furry head. In the next instant the
events of the day penetrated her foggy mind, and
her eyes shot open. She also sneezed.

"Good," Graham said, poking his head in the
door. "You're awake. Stay put and I'll get you something to eat."

"But . . ."

"I'll be right back."

Autumn looked down at herself, then gasped in
dismay and yanked the blankets up to her chin. A
quick glance at the clock on the nightstand told
her it was nearly five o'clock. She'd slept the afternoon away. And Graham Kimble was roaming
around in her apartment! She shoved the pillow up

behind her and sat up, tucking the blankets tightly under her arms to cover her breasts.

A minute later Graham entered the room, carrying a tray. He was dressed in faded jeans and a black V-neck sweater over a white cotton shirt. Her gaze swept over him, missing no detail of the way the jeans molded to his hips and legs, or of how broad his shoulders appeared under the soft material of his sweater.

"Hi!" he said, smiling. "Soup's on." He placed the tray across her legs, then pulled the chair close to the bed and sat down. "How are you feeling, Agatha?" he asked gently.

How was she feeling? she repeated silently, staring into his warm brown eyes. Like a princess. Like someone who was cherished, cared for. Like a woman in love, that was how she felt.

A great joy filled her. She had never doubted that she would someday love. Her earlier disastrous affair had been a growing experience, a lesson in learning the difference between love and physical attraction. Now love had come in all its magnificence in the form of this man, Graham Kimble. It wasn't frightening, it was exciting, making her feel more alive than ever before. Everything seemed sharper, more vivid. Even nursing a cold, she felt beautiful. Beautiful and feminine, and in love.

"I feel much better," she said, smiling at him.

Time stopped. Neither moved nor spoke. They simply gazed at each other as though they were meeting again after many years apart. There was a new awareness between them, a heightening of the senses. Autumn felt the tension building between them and caught her breath in excited anticipation.

Then Graham spoke. In a low, sensual, velvety voice, he said, "Agatha."

Autumn felt as if her heart were splintering into a million pieces. She bent her head to hide the tears that sprang quickly to her eyes and gripped the edge of the tray with trembling hands.

"Try to eat, okay?" he said. "There's soup, juice, and toast. Just do the best you can. I'll go clean up the mess I made in the kitchen, then come back and check on you."

She nodded, then watched with tear-filled eyes as he left the room. Oh, how she loved him. She loved a man who didn't know her, a man who was infatuated with another woman. He was enthralled by Agatha's intelligence, her fondness for historical trivia, her sense of humor that prompted her to laugh in the middle of a raging downpour.

Wait a minute! Autumn thought suddenly. *She* was intelligent, liked history, and had a sense of humor. All those things were true of her, Autumn. They didn't belong exclusively to Agatha. The only glaring difference between the two women was their outward appearance!

What if, Autumn mused, taking a bite of toast, she actually became Agatha! Oh, how crazy! But was it? She would be sacrificing nothing more than a closet full of pretty clothes and a makeup kit. Her values, goals, hopes, and dreams wouldn't change. She'd see the light and switch her views to match Graham's about preserving the environment, and agree that squirrels were the cutest animals in the woods, and dress like a frump. Oh, ugh.

No, it would never work, she told herself, because it would all be a lie, and it would catch up with her. Bish Terzoni was a perfect example of how quickly Agatha's cover could be blown. Graham had to be told the truth. But what he had to be made to see was that the differences between Agatha and Autumn were minimal, of little consequence. She'd chuck her gorgeous, expensive wardrobe right out the window if it meant having the love of Graham Kimble!

But when should she tell him the teeny, tiny, insignificant newsflash that Agatha Stanton had never been born? That was the tricky part. The timing had to be perfect because oh, dear heaven, she didn't want to lose her Graham!

"I'm back," he said, striding into the room. "Hey, good for you. You ate every bite."

"I did?" She looked at the tray. "I'll be darned, I did. I'm feeling much better, too. You know, Graham," she went on as he placed the tray on the dresser, "I really appreciate your fussing over me like this."

"Well," he said, sitting down in the chair, "it's my fault that you got sick. Truth of the matter is, though, I want to be here with you. I'd go out of my mind in my apartment worrying about you being alone when you don't feel well. When do you expect Autumn to show up?"

She frowned. "Not until next week. I think. Maybe it will be longer than that. I'm really not sure at this point."

"Where is she?"

"Taking care of some important business. Is my nose red? I must look awful."

He smiled. "You look just fine. You . . . um, do intend to wear your hair like that from now on, don't you? It's very attractive."

"Yes," she said, fluffing her hair with one hand. "I believe I will leave it loose. You know, you do wonderful things for those jeans. I can't decide if I like you better dressed like that or in your spiffy suits."

"I didn't think you paid much attention to clothes, Agatha. What I mean is, you don't seem to follow the latest fashions."

"Well, I . . ."

"Which is fine," he rushed on. "I was just thinking of your comfort, that's all."

"My comfort?"

"Yes. You stopped your teeth from aching by removing your glasses, and I'm sure that tight bun was rather rough on your head. Seems to me that perhaps some lighter-weight shoes would be easier on your feet. Right? Then there's that dress you wore today. It was lovely, really nice, but it did prove to be a problem once it got wet."

"True," she said, nodding and frowning slightly. What was Graham doing? she wondered. If she didn't know better, she'd think he was making a pitch for her to do something constructive about her appearance. No, that didn't make sense. He'd spent too much time telling Agatha to stay exactly as she was. She was reading too much into idle chitchat. It would be music to her ears if he told her to shape up, but it wasn't going to happen.

"Anyway," he said, "comfort is important."

"It certainly is."

"Now, take these jeans . . ."

Oh, she'd be happy to, she thought merrily. She'd be delighted to take those jeans right off his body. Shame on her!

"They're soft, comfortable, easy to wear. Maybe you should get yourself a pair." He leaned forward and took her hands between his. "Sweaters are nice, too. You'd be sensational in a sweater the color of your eyes." What was he saying? he asked himself. Agatha would look terrific in a sweater that mirrored the green of her eyes and molded to her beautiful breasts. Dammit, he was hating this! Every guy in the city would ogle her. He was creating a Betty Bazooms out of his wonderful Harriet Housewife!

"Jeans and sweaters," Autumn said thoughtfully. Why not? What were a few more added to the dozen she owned? But Graham was confusing her again. Since he had made reference to his own attire, she had the distinct impression he was referring to her purchasing snug-fitting jeans and sweaters, not the oversized garments he'd seen her wearing. What, in heaven's name, was he trying to do? "Jeans and sweaters?" she repeated.

"Comfort first, remember?"

"Well, I couldn't wear jeans to your office."

"Maybe not, but we could get you some other things, too."

"We?"

"Would you prefer to go shopping with Autumn?"

"No! I think a shopping spree with you would be very enjoyable, Graham. It's just that . . . well . . ."

"Yes?"

"I'm rather confused. You've placed a lot of emphasis on my staying just as I am, and now you're inferring I should get a new wardrobe."

"For comfort," he said, moving to sit on the edge of the bed. His action disturbed Cricket, and the cat jumped off the bed and dashed out of the room. "Don't think for a minute that I don't find you attractive just as you are. We'll pick things that are exactly right for you. It'll be fun, an adventure. Okay?"

"Okay," she said, smiling at him warmly.

He smiled back, then both smiles slowly faded as they gazed at each other. Desire tingled through Autumn as she sat mesmerized by Graham's dark eyes. Tension wove around them, a sensuality that seemed to pull them closer. Slowly, Autumn lifted her hands to cradle Graham's face, and the blankets slid to her waist.

His gaze flickered over her breasts, then returned to her face. His body was stiff as he willed himself not to move, not to grab her and claim her mouth with his.

Autumn sensed his struggle for control, and her heart nearly burst with love. Feeling both excitement and serenity, she leaned forward and pressed her lips to his.

With a groan that rumbled up from his throat, he gathered her close to his chest, his tongue delving deep into her mouth as her arms circled his neck. The ember of desire within them burst into a raging flame of need.

He drew a shuddering breath, then trailed a ribbon of kisses down her throat and across the tops of her aching breasts, creating a path of tantalizing sensations as he went.

"Let me see you," he said, his voice hoarse. "Lord, how I want to see you."

She moved back, and with slightly trembling hands he slid the straps of her nightgown down her arms. The bodice fell to her waist.

He closed his eyes tight for a moment, then opened them again to gaze at her breasts. He filled his hands with their lushness and lowered his head to draw one rosy bud into his mouth.

She tilted her head back, her lashes drifting down as she savored the sensations spiraling through her. Her fingers burrowed into Graham's thick hair, urging him closer, urging him to take more of her. His mouth found her other breast, his tongue flickering over the nipple, bringing it to an aching tautness.

"Oh, Graham," she whispered, her breathing erratic as her heart battered against her ribs.

"I want you, Agatha," he murmured. "There aren't words to tell you how much I desire you."

Agatha, her mind echoed. He wanted Agatha; she was Autumn. She was living a lie, but she didn't care. She loved him. Later, she would sort it all through, find the solution to her dilemma, and carefully explain to Graham how innocently the deception had begun. Later. But now there was no thought beyond the moment and the man, no need greater than the one to take him into herself and rejoice in their union.

"Yes," she said, her voice unsteady. "Yes, Graham, I want you to make love to me."

He gazed directly into her eyes as if seeking the

path to her soul. His mind warred with his body, even as overwhelming desire made it almost impossible to think. Never had he craved a woman the way he did her. And she wanted him. The message was there in her emerald eyes, an invitation to him to quell the fire raging in both of them. What they would share would be a celebration, a journey of ecstasy and fulfillment. He would assure her pleasure first, before seeking release for his aching body. It would be perfect for her.

He kissed her gently, reverently, as though to seal with trust the decision they had made together. Then he drew her nightgown down and away from her slender body.

"Beautiful," he murmured. "So very, very beautiful."

He stood up and removed his clothes. Autumn was hardly breathing as she watched Graham disrobe. His body shone with a fine film of perspiration, transforming his skin into glistening golden beauty. His broad chest was covered with tawny curls, his shoulders and arms corded with muscles. His manhood spoke boldly of his need and desire for her. He was magnificent.

"Graham."

The seductive whisper of her voice seemed to caress him, and he shuddered as he stretched out next to her. He skimmed his hand over the flat plane of her stomach, down to her thighs, then back up to her breasts. Where his hand had traveled his lips followed in a tantalizing, sensuous journey that brought a moan of pleasure from her lips. She clutched his arms almost desperately and murmured his name over and over.

With every ounce of control he could muster, Graham held himself back, and his muscles trembled from the effort of his restraint. Every thought in his mind, every beat of his racing heart, every whisper from his soul was for this woman. Good Lord, how he loved her!

"Oh, Graham, please!" she cried.

"Yes!"

He came to her with strength tempered by gentleness, and she received him with love. She arched her back to meet him, to urge him deeper and deeper inside her. They moved together, striving to please each other, to reach that magic place beyond reality.

When she felt herself teetering on the edge, Autumn cried out to Graham. He answered her with a powerful thrust, and together they fell into ecstasy. Rocketing spasms swept through both of them, and what one felt, so did the other. It was a joining of bodies, and of souls. It was heaven. They lingered in that place known only to themselves, then drifted back, sated, contented, fulfilled.

Graham shifted away, then drew Autumn to his side, sifting his fingers through the silky strands of her hair.

"You were wonderful," he said, his voice low. "Thank you for trusting me so much. Things have happened very quickly between us, but it's so good, so right. Agatha, I love you. I truly love you."

No! Autumn screamed silently. Oh, please, no! He couldn't love Agatha! Why hadn't he waited for her, for Autumn? "No," she said, not realizing she had spoken out loud.

"Don't be frightened," he said, wrapping his arm

around her waist. "I can feel you tensing. There's nothing for you to fear, Agatha. I'll never hurt you. Never. Do you know that I didn't believe in love before I met you? I knew I was ready for a change in my life, but I never dreamed it would include falling in love."

"But you hardly know me."

"Let me worry about that. I don't want you to feel rushed or pressured by my expressing my feelings for you. It's just important to me that I be honest with you."

"Yes, of course. Honesty," she said miserably. "That means a lot to you."

"It's a solid foundation on which to build a relationship."

"Graham, my life is very complicated right now. I'm so close to obtaining my degree, and I can't allow anything to interfere with that."

"I know, and I intend to be a paragon of patience while you work toward your goal," he said. And while she emerged from her cocoon, he added to himself. He was going to help her pick out some lovely new clothes, help her see how beautiful she was. And then what?

They lay in silence, lost in their own thoughts. Autumn trailed a fingertip over Graham's chest as she tried desperately to sort through the jumble in her mind. The lovemaking she had shared with Graham had been the most wonderful experience in her life. He had staked his total claim on her, heart, body, mind, and soul. She couldn't tell him the truth, not now, not in the aftermath of their union. The moment was too precious to be tarnished by the cold reality of what she had done.

Lies, she thought. So many lies. Her intentions had been innocent, but those little white lies now wielded the power to shatter her happiness. So much was at stake. Graham loved Agatha. What he didn't realize was that he was also in love with Autumn. But he was giving every indication that he was taking Agatha's appearance under his control. Love was not blind! He saw Agatha's potential beauty and had decided to do something about it. In any other man she'd resent his taking charge like that, but in this case it would accomplish exactly what had to be done. Good-bye, Agatha; hello, Autumn. Then she would carefully explain to Graham that she had withheld the truth to show him that she loved him so much she had been willing to be whoever would make him happy. If the new clothes turned him off, she'd go back to the frumpy ones, no questions asked.

Yes, it made sense! It was a sound plan. The final outcome would be that Graham would realize how deeply she loved him, and they would ride blissfully off into the sunset together.

"How nice," she murmured wistfully.

"What is?"

"Life."

"True." He brushed his lips over her forehead. "But mine is going to be very short if I don't get something to eat. I'm starving."

"I'll make you something."

"Don't be silly. You're sick in bed with a cold."

"That nap fixed me up. Besides, you didn't seem too concerned about my germs a little while ago."

"It wasn't your germs I was concentrating on," he said, sliding his hand up over her stomach to her breasts. He lowered his head to kiss the soft flesh. "You're so beautiful," he said.

"So are you," she said, twining her fingers through the curly hair on his chest.

"Don't misunderstand, Agatha. I don't love you for your beauty. I mean, I'm not complaining that you're the loveliest woman I've ever made love to. What I'm trying to say is, I highly respect your intelligence, values, accomplishments. Outward appearance is of no importance."

"I see," she said, her hand creeping lower.

"In fact, if you'd prefer not to go shopping for new clothes, we'll just forget the whole thing. It was only for your comfort, anyway. Say the word, and we won't go."

"Oh, no, I want to go. It'll be fun."

"Well, if you're sure. I wouldn't want to force you to—" He gasped. "You are driving me crazy!"

"Me?" she said, then flicked her tongue in a lazy circle over his chest.

"Agatha!"

"Yes, Graham?" She gazed up at him with a look of pure innocence on her face.

His mouth swept down onto hers, smothering the bubble of laughter that threatened to escape from her lips. The kiss was urgent, igniting their fiery passions once more. They drank of the sweetness of each other as though parched, their hands roaming, exploring the mysteries of one another's bodies. When they came together Autumn's body seemed to explode. She clung to Graham as again they discovered ecstasy.

As they slowly drifted back to reality, they held each other in silence, unable to find the words to

"alluring"..."inspiring"...
"irresistible"...

Loveswept

EXAMINE 4 LOVESWEPT NOVELS FOR

15 Days FREE!

Turn page for details

America's most popular, most compelling romance novels...

Loveswept

Here, at last...love stories that really involve you! Fresh, finely crafted novels with story lines so believable you'll feel you're actually living them!

Read a Loveswept novel and you'll experience all the very real feelings of two people as they discover and build an involved relationship: laughing, crying, learning and loving. Characters you can relate to... exciting places to visit...unexpected plot twists...all in all, exciting romances that satisfy your mind and delight your heart.

And now you can be sure you'll never, ever miss a single Loveswept title by enrolling in our special reader's home delivery service. A service that will bring all four new Loveswept romances published every month into your home—and deliver them to you *before* they appear in the bookstores!

Examine 4 Loveswept Novels for

15 Days FREE!

To introduce you to this fabulous service, you'll get four brand-new Loveswept releases not yet in the bookstores. These four exciting new titles are yours to examine for 15 days without obligation to buy. Keep them if you wish for just $9.95 plus postage and handling and any applicable sales tax.

SEND NO MONEY NOW.
RETURN THIS
POSTAGE-PAID CARD TODAY!

FREE TRIAL/HOME DELIVERY ORDER CARD

Loveswept
Bantam Books, P.O. Box 985, Hicksville, NY 11802

☐ Please send me four new romances for a 15-day FREE examination.
If I keep them, I will pay just $9.95 plus postage and handling and any
applicable sales tax and you will enter my name on your preferred cus-
tomer list to receive all four new Loveswept novels published each month
before they are released to the bookstores—always on the same 15-day
free examination basis.

20123

Name_____

Address_____

City_____

State_____Zip_____

My Guarantee: I am never required to buy any shipment unless I wish. I
may preview each shipment for 15 days. If I don't want it, I simply return the
shipment within 15 days and owe nothing for it.   F12

BUSINESS REPLY MAIL

FIRST-CLASS MAIL   PERMIT NO. 2456   HICKSVILLE, NY

Postage will be paid by addressee

Loveswept

Bantam Books
P.O. Box 985
Hicksville, NY 11802

express the magnificence of their loving. Finally, Graham kissed her deeply and moved away.

"Incredible," he said.

"Yes, you are," she said as her eyes drifted closed. "Absolutely incredible."

"I love you."

And I love you, she said silently. But she couldn't speak those words until all the shadows of deception were gone, until she was Autumn. The declaration of love was not Agatha's to make.

"Well," he said, swinging his legs off the bed, "I'm going to scramble up a few eggs. Want some?"

"No, thanks. I'll join you, though, and have a cup of tea."

"All right." He pulled on his jeans. "Put on something warm. You still sound full of cold."

"I—aaa-*choo!*"

"I rest my case." He finished dressing, kissed her quickly, and strode from the room.

Autumn slipped her nightgown over her head, then walked to the closet, where her favorite faded blue terry-cloth robe hung. She'd had it for years, and it was soft and comfortable, as well as being rather out of shape. Perfect for Agatha, she thought.

In the kitchen she fed Cricket, set water on to boil for her tea, then sat down at the glass-topped table to watch Graham cook. He moved with a sensuous ease, and she found herself staring at his expressive hands as he cracked the eggs, remembering how those hands had explored her body. . . .

Agatha hadn't said it, Graham thought as he poured the eggs into the frying pan. She hadn't said that she loved him. He'd waited for the words, hoping, praying they'd come, but she'd been silent. Their lovemaking had been fantastic. She had given of herself totally, trustingly, holding nothing back. He wanted to ask her to marry him but couldn't until she told him she loved him. So, he'd wait. He had no other choice. He'd help her turn into a beautiful butterfly, cross his fingers, and wait.

"You seem to know your way around a kitchen," she said.

"My mom insisted I learn how to cook. My sister had to pass tests on changing a tire, too. None of this male or female stuff in our house. You should have seen me the time I tried to sew a button on my shirt. I poked every one of my fingers, but I got no sympathy."

"Did you get the button on?"

He laughed. "Damn right. By then, my folks had a ten-dollar bet riding on it. It was a matter of pride."

"Your family sounds very nice."

"They are. My parents are retired now, living down in Malibu. My sister is married and has a baby. They live in Seattle. I realize you only have Autumn, but someday, well . . . Sure you don't want some eggs?"

"No, I had plenty to eat with all that food you put on the tray." Oh, darn, she thought. Another one of her lies had popped up. Enough was enough. She couldn't take any more of this! She was going to tell Graham the truth right now. "Graham," she said as he sat down opposite her, "in order to gather data for my thesis, I have had to do very extensive research."

"Yes, I can imagine," he said. "Psychology is pretty heavy-duty stuff."

"Yes, well, I've spent many hours in the library collecting information to prove my theory."

"Theory?"

"The theme of my thesis is that women in society reap what they sow. There are exceptions, of course, but I feel confident that I will present a sound case."

"Good for you," he said, nodding. "So, you're implying that if women present themselves in a certain way, men are going to react accordingly?"

"Exactly. My research dates back to the turn of the century. But . . . well, you see, I wanted some examples from today's society, things I had experienced firsthand."

"Don't you want your tea? The water's boiled."

"What? No, that's all right. Graham, in the interests of research I dressed up like a nun, went into a sleazy bar, and—"

"You did what?" he roared. "Alone? You went alone?"

"Well, yes. You see, I knew the men would treat a nun with respect, and they did."

"I can't believe this!" He smacked the table with his hand. "Don't you realize what could have happened to you? I thought you were smarter than that! There are men in this world who don't follow any rules at all! What other screwy things did you do for your damnable research? No, don't tell me, I don't want to know. All I wish to hear is that you've finished gathering your ever-famous data."

"Yes, I have, but I don't see what you're getting so hyper about!"

"Agatha," he said, his voice gentling, "please try to understand. I've never been in love before, and I'm being swamped by emotions that are foreign to me. I want to protect you, keep you from harm. I'm sure I'll get a handle on all of this so that I don't smother you. But in the meantime, have mercy, okay? Don't tell me any more gruesome tales about what you did to collect information for your thesis. My nervous system just can't take it right now."

"Just one more story?" she asked hopefully, leaning toward him.

"No!"

"Oh." She slumped back in her chair. "Darn."

"We'll share everything, Agatha, but I think most of the past should be left alone. I'm sure you wouldn't want to hear about . . . Never mind."

"About what?" she asked, leaning forward again. "Your women? I bet you lost count somewhere along the line."

"Agatha, please! All that is behind me now. We should make a pact to move forward together, not dwell on old news."

"Sort of a blank check forgiving all that happened before the day we met?"

"Something like that, yes."

"Including the day we met?" The day Agatha was born, and the charade began?

"Whatever," he said, lifting a shoulder in a shrug. "That's a good idea. That wipes out Joyce St. James."

"Who? Oh, yes, Joyce. I don't know about this,

Graham. There's something very important that I need to tell you."

"Regarding your research gathering?"

"Yes."

"No. I'll get an ulcer to match the one Bish claims I'm giving him. Whatever you did, you did, but I don't want to hear about it. I'm sure your thesis will be brilliant, Agatha. Let's leave it at that."

"Not good," she said, shaking her head. "Not good at all."

"Trust me," he said, getting to his feet and carrying his empty plate to the sink. "I think you should go back to bed now and rest. As much as I hate to leave you, I'd better get home and draft a preliminary report for Fisher. Do you have those notes?"

"Yes, they're in my purse. I'll get them."

In the living room, Graham pulled Autumn into his embrace. She circled his waist with her arms and smiled up at him.

"I really don't want to go," he said, "but you need your sleep."

"I slept all afternoon."

"Colds are very tiring. I don't want you coming into the office tomorrow if you're not feeling well. Promise me you'll take good care of yourself, Agatha."

"Yes, I will."

"You're not sorry we made love, are you? Please don't have any regrets about what happened between us. I love you very much, Agatha Stanton."

He lowered his head to claim her mouth, and Autumn melted against him, relishing the taste, the feel, the heat of Graham Kimble. Their tongues met, and their soft moans drifted through the air. Flames of desire licked through Autumn once again, and her knees trembled. The room began to fade into a hazy mist, then Graham lifted his head.

"If I don't leave now, I won't leave at all," he said, his breathing labored.

"Stay, Graham."

"No. I feel guilty enough that you got so sick. You really should rest, and I have to do that report. If I stay, I'll make love to you until dawn. Good night, Agatha." He brushed his lips lightly over hers, picked up the notebook, then walked to the door. "Sleep well, my love," he said quietly, and left the apartment.

Autumn stared at the closed door for several minutes, then walked into the kitchen to make the cup of tea. After turning the burner back on under the kettle, she sank onto a chair, crossed her arms on top of the table, and sighed.

She still hadn't told Graham the truth about Agatha, she thought guiltily. He'd flipped out about her nun disguise and the jaunt to the bar, and that had been that. She believed in Graham's philosophy that what had gone before should be left alone. She certainly didn't want to hear about his bed-hopping escapades, nor did she condemn him for them. He was a virile man. Heat rose to her cheeks. Was he ever! The problem was that what she had tried to confess spilled over into their today and tomorrows.

She was, she supposed, back to her original plan. She would remain as Agatha for now and bide her time. She'd gauge Graham's reactions to the clothes she bought on the shopping trip and try to determine when and to what extent Autumn could emerge. Then, and only then, could she tell Graham of her love for him.

After drinking the tea, Autumn walked slowly back into the bedroom and stretched out on the bed, burying her face in the pillow that held the lingering aroma of Graham Kimble.

Six

Graham studied the blueprints on the drafting board, then nodded in approval. Bish's plans were finished, and they were perfect. This called for a celebration!

He walked to the outer office, where Agatha was typing a letter. She heard him approach and turned to smile up at him, her hair swinging in a strawberry-blond swirl around her shoulders.

"Hi," he said. "I've hardly had a minute to speak to you all day. How are you feeling?"

"Fine. My cold is completely gone," she said.

"You look fine," he said. Much better, in fact, he decided. He really liked her hair like that. And while the baggy black-and-orange-striped dress was horrendous, she was wearing black patent-leather shoes with three-inch heels that did fantastic things for her legs. Her regular shoes, she had told him, were still in the trunk of his car, so she'd borrowed a pair of Autumn's. Her hair and feet were sensational. The problem was everything in between!

"Agatha," he said, "I just finished Bish's plans ahead of schedule. What do you say we go out tonight to celebrate?"

"I'd love to, but I can't."

"Oh?"

"I have patients to see tonight; I am paired with a certified psychologist for group therapy sessions. It's an internship of sorts that's a necessary part of the work on my doctorate. Tonight will conclude my required number of hours."

"No kidding? Then you'll have something to celebrate, too. We'll have to plan a special outing. Well, I'll go call Bish and tell him his blueprints are ready."

"Thank you for the invitation."

"Sure," he said, smiling at her. "We'll just take a rain check."

She'd settle for a kiss for now, Autumn thought as Graham went back into his office. He'd kissed her when he'd picked her up that morning to drive her to the office, and she had melted in his arms. Then he'd been so busy, he'd hardly come up for air. Well, the man was a dedicated architect. And she was starting to sound like a sex maniac! But she loved him so much. Just the thought of him got her all in a dither. And when he smiled at her, kissed and touched her, she all but swooned.

Being in love, she mused, was fantastic, a great place to be. It would help immensely if the man in question loved *her* instead of dippy Agatha, but she was working on that, slowly but surely.

At five o'clock, Graham came out of his office with a cardboard tube under his arm. He set it on Autumn's desk, then walked around to her chair, extending his hand to her.

"Come here, my lady," he said.

Hooray! Autumn cheered silently as she moved into his embrace.

He brushed his mouth across hers, then slid his tongue slowly, seductively, along her bottom lip. Her lips parted and her eyes drifted closed as she anticipated the moment when his mouth would totally claim hers, and the now familiar sensations of desire would stir deep within her. She leaned heavily against him, but his lips wandered to her cheeks, her eyelids, down the slender column of her throat.

She inhaled the lingering aroma of his aftershave as she gripped his shoulders. He murmured her name in his voice of dark velvet, and her knees went weak. His mouth was sweet torture as it skimmed over her flushed skin, and she was sure if he didn't kiss her, really kiss her, this instant she would die. She sought his mouth with hers, and with a moan he crushed her to him. The kiss was rough and urgent, weaving an inescapable web of sensuality about them. She clung to him, unable to stand on her own, and his arms tightened about her.

"Oh, Agatha," he said, gasping, when he finally lifted his head.

"Graham." She sighed and snuggled against him.

"How would you feel about making love on top of your desk? Tacky. Forget I asked. But dammit, Agatha, I want you!"

Desks were nice, Autumn thought dreamily. Oh, good grief! "I . . ." she started, then drew a steadying breath. "I really must go. I mustn't be late for my appointments."

"Okay," he said, frowning.

He slid his hands down her arms to catch her fingers, then lifted each hand in turn to place a gentle kiss on the palm. She shivered in sensuous delight.

"I guess you'll want to take your car," he said.

"Yes. I appreciate your picking me up this morning, but I do need my car tonight. I'll see you in the morning, Graham."

"Yeah. You go ahead. I'll close up here."

She kissed him quickly, smiled, then picked up her purse and left the office. Graham sank back onto the edge of the desk and gave his body a firm directive to cool off. A deep frown knitted his eyebrows together as he stared into space.

He would have done it, he thought. He would have made love to that woman on the top of her desk! Where was his maturity, his control and restraint? It had flown the coop when he fell in love with Agatha Stanton. Love was strange. It blew his mind and had his body begging for mercy.

"Well, hell," he muttered. He was going to go meet Bish and have a drink. A lot of drinks!

Two hours later, Bish frowned and pushed Graham's plate toward him.

"Eat something, Cracker," he said. "You're getting smashed."

"That's the plan," Graham said sullenly.

"Well, the waiter is hovering around like he wants this table. Let's go over to the bar on the other side, and you can tell me what's bugging you. All you've said since I met you here is, 'Hi, Bish, how's life?' Come on."

"All right."

In the dimly lit bar, Graham sank heavily onto the leather banquette seat of a booth as Bish slid in across from him. Graham ordered drinks from a passing cocktail waitress, then sighed.

"Okay, Cracker," Bish said, "what's wrong?"

"I'm losing it, Bish. My mind is mush. I've never been so confused in my entire life."

"About what?"

"Love. Agatha. Everything. By the way, I'm in love with Agatha. Did I tell you that? No, guess not. Well, I am. I'm in love with Agatha Stanton."

"Dammit," Bish muttered.

"What?"

"Nothing. Go on with your story. I can't say that you're the happiest man in love that I've ever seen."

"That's due to my mental confusion. You see, Bish, I had every intention of accepting and appreciating Agatha exactly as she was. A Betty Bazooms she's not, but that was fine. But then, well, I began to see her potential beauty. It's all there, just below the surface of those awful clothes she wears."

"And?"

"I started making little suggestions to her, like wearing her hair loose, getting some new clothes, stuff like that. She was very receptive to everything I said. That's when my brain turned into scrambled eggs."

"Why?"

"I figured it would be really shabby of me not to help her be as beautiful as she could be. She has that right, you know what I mean? Now we get to the part where I scare my socks off. I'm afraid she'll come out of the ether, realize she's gorgeous, and start enjoying the attention she'll get from other men."

"You can hold your own. You're as good as the competition, Cracker."

"Maybe, maybe not. I win some, I lose some. It's never mattered before." He paused as the waitress set their drinks down and left. "I love Agatha, Bish. I can't handle the thought of losing her to another man. And there's something else, too," he added miserably.

"More?"

"Yeah. What if, just suppose, I'm subconsciously trying to spiff Agatha up for myself? What if I haven't been accepting her appearance at all? Oh, that's so lousy I can't stand it. I'd be a low-life from the word go."

"Take it easy. You're really getting upset here. You're also being too hard on yourself."

"I'm a scum, a louse, a—"

"Would you knock that off and listen to me? You're helping Agatha discover the full potential of her beauty, right? But you're questioning your motives, right? Right. There's only one solution to this."

"I'll have myself strung up by the thumbs," Graham said, and took a deep swallow of his drink.

"No! You go on emotional hold."

"Huh?"

"You're too close to all of this, Cracker. You can't pursue your love for Agatha while you're showing her how to come out of her shell. You've got to put your love in cold storage until her transformation is complete. Then you sort of start over, view things fresh, just as she'll be doing."

"Are you nuts? I can't turn my feelings off like a faucet!"

"It's the only way. Love has to be nurtured, given a man's undivided attention. You're torn in so many directions that every aspect of your life will suffer. Pull back, do one thing at a time. For now, concentrate on the transformation of Agatha Stanton into a beautiful woman."

"I don't know about this."

"Trust me. I'm positive that things will fall into place once plain Agatha is out of the picture. I'll shut up now. You sit there and think about what I said."

"Okay," Graham said, squinting at the ceiling. "I'm thinking."

"And I'm praying," Bish said under his breath.

At that moment Autumn entered the bar with an attractive woman in her forties. They sat down at a booth and ordered drinks.

"I can't believe it," Autumn said. "My group therapy sessions are over. I can't thank you enough, Dr. Wagner, for all your patience and assistance over the past months."

"It was a pleasure working with you, Autumn.

You have a natural compassion for people, you're sensitive, intelligent . . . well, the list goes on and on. I'll complete my report and forward it on to your doctoral adviser. Just think, once you've completed your thesis and it's been accepted, you'll be Dr. Autumn Stanton."

"Oh, that sounds so wonderful!"

"So, bring me up to date on your thesis. Have you gathered all the data you need?"

As Autumn began discussing her research, on the other side of the room Graham discovered that tilting his head back and squinting made him slightly dizzy. He gingerly straightened, opened his eyes, then his mouth, but no sound came out.

"Agatha," he finally managed to croak.

"What?" Bish said.

"She's sitting right over there in that booth!"

Bish turned to look and cringed. "Uh-oh," he said.

Graham leaned forward and frowned. "What is she wearing?" he muttered.

"A dress. Want another drink?"

"A green dress, the exact shade of her eyes, and it fits her! Damn, does it ever fit her. Look at that! It hugs her breasts, her waist . . . What in the hell does she think she's doing?"

"Cracker, calm down!"

"Like hell I will!" He lunged to his feet and started across the room. Bish was right behind him.

". . . still compiling my notes," Autumn was saying when she happened to look up. "Oh, good Lord!"

"What's wrong?" Dr. Wagner asked.

"Oh, please, Dr. Wagner," Autumn said, "whatever happens in the next few minutes, just play along, okay? It's more important to me than I can ever begin to tell you."

"Yes, all right, but what—"

"Agatha!" Graham said, coming to a rather unsteady stop at their table. "You're even wearing makeup. That's green eye shadow, and you have on lipstick, and—"

"I don't believe we've met," she interrupted. "I'm Autumn Stanton." She smiled sweetly, though her heart was thudding painfully.

"Dammit, Agatha," Graham roared, "I demand to know why you're dressed like— You're who?"

"Autumn Stanton, Agatha's cousin."

"Cousin? What cousin?" Dr. Wagner said. "Oh, of course, your cousin!"

"Hello, Autumn," Bish said, smiling over Graham's shoulder. "I'm Bish Terzoni. I guess the gang's all here, huh? This is Graham Kimble, by the way."

"Mr. Kimble," Autumn said, nodding. "It's a pleasure. I understand that Agatha is working for you temporarily."

"What?" He blinked once, slowly. "Oh, yeah, she is. You two could be twins! You look exactly alike. Well, there are a few differences, but . . ."

"Would you care to join us?" Autumn asked. "This is Dr. Lisa Wagner."

"Wouldn't miss this for the world," Bish said, sliding in beside Dr. Wagner. "Close your mouth, Cracker, and sit down next to Autumn."

"Oh, sure," he said, doing as instructed, his gaze riveted on Autumn. "This is rather disconcerting.

You're everything what I imagined Agatha would look like if she . . . what I mean is . . ."

"Some men might find Agatha's unpretentious appearance refreshing, Mr. Kimble," Autumn said. "I take it that you prefer a more modern woman?"

"He's taking it under advisement at this point in time," Bish said.

"Who are you?" Dr. Wagner asked. "His lawyer?"

"Close," Bish said, nodding. "I'm Graham's best friend. He cares deeply for Agatha and feels that perhaps she should be encouraged to enhance her natural beauty."

"Hear, hear," Autumn said, lifting her glass. "I'm all for that. You agree, don't you, Dr. Wagner? Of course you do. Agatha has a whole world waiting for her out there."

"She does?" Graham said, sitting bolt upward.

"No!" Bish said quickly, glaring at Autumn. "A new wardrobe, that's all, and a little makeup. Autumn wasn't referring to a world of men or the fast lane."

"Heavens, no!" Autumn said, covering her heart with her hand. "I know Agatha as well as I know myself. We don't indulge in the party life. We believe in loyalty, apple pie, and the American way."

"I can't believe she actually said that," Dr. Wagner mumbled into her glass. Bish glared at her, too.

"Isn't this something, Cracker?" Bish said, smiling brightly. "Two women who not only look alike, but have the same viewpoints, values, all that jazz. Intelligence, too, I'll bet. The only difference between them is their choice of clothes. How do you think Agatha would look in that dress Autumn is wearing?"

"Sensational," Graham said, looking directly into Autumn's eyes. "Just sensational."

"Thank you, Graham," she said softly as she fell prey to the mesmerizing depths of his dark eyes.

"Let's dance," Bish said, grabbing Dr. Wagner's hand and hauling her out of the booth.

"Something very strange is happening here," Graham said, shaking his head and tearing his gaze from Autumn's. "I think I'm drunk."

"Why? What's wrong?"

"Your voice, your perfume, the way you look at me, it's all Agatha."

Tell him! Autumn's mind screamed. Right now! Tell him! "Graham," she said, taking a deep breath, "I *am* Agatha. And I'm pretty. You don't mind if I'm attractive, do you? If so, I'll gladly go back to wearing the other—"

"Damn you!" he swore, and slid out of the booth. "You really had me fooled there for a minute. I thought you were a sweet, wholesome woman like Agatha, but you're not! You're just a typical Betty Bazooms out for a good time. You don't even care that you're trying to hit on your own cousin's man! Well, no soap, Miss Autumn Stanton. I'm not one damn bit interested in you. It's Agatha I care about, so you can just forget it!"

"No, Graham, wait! You don't understand! I'm trying to explain that I—"

"I got the message loud and clear. No sale, kid. I'm spoken for." He turned and strode toward the door.

"Oh, darn it!" Autumn said, smacking the table with her hand. "Oh, dammit!"

In the next moment a scowling Bish returned to the table with Lisa Wagner in tow.

"What the hell happened?" Bish yelled, causing several heads to turn in his direction.

"Could we sit down?" Lisa suggested.

"I told Graham I was Agatha," Autumn said.

"I'm sitting down," Lisa said. She sat, then yanked on Bish's arm.

"And?" Bish said, plopping down and leaning toward Autumn.

"He got furious," she said, throwing up her hands. "He thought Autumn was making a play for him. You know, doing a cutesy thing by saying she'd be Agatha for him since he seemed to prefer her. He thinks I'm a hussy," she wailed.

"Oh, dear," Lisa said.

"Oh, hell," Bish said.

"Autumn," Lisa said, "Bish explained everything while we were dancing. You told Graham the truth and he refused to believe you?"

"Yes," Autumn said, nodding miserably. "The way he was looking at me I just melted. I couldn't do it anymore. I had to tell him, but he took it all wrong. He despises Autumn. Oh, what am I going to do? I love Graham so much."

"You do?" Bish said. "No kidding? You really do?"

"Do you have a hearing problem? Yes, I love him, but he loves Agatha! He told her . . . me . . . that he loves her. He was also starting to hint that he might prefer Agatha dressed a little more attractively, and I agreed. I decided that his love is worth more than fancy clothes. Maybe it's hopelessly unliberated of me, but I'll dress in whichever manner pleases Graham."

"I'll be damned," Bish said. "That's really nice."

"Bish, aren't you paying attention?" Autumn said, smacking the table again.

He jumped. "Sorry. Did I miss something?"

"Only the fact that my willingness to conform to Graham's wishes was to be my proof of how much I love him. I then intended to tell him how Agatha came to exist, and that I'm really Autumn."

"Not bad," Bish said, nodding in approval.

"Not good," Lisa said. "Graham has now met Autumn, and obviously thinks she's a naughty girl. I would guess that Agatha will be even more appealing to Graham now, perhaps to the point he'll want to protect her from Autumn's wanton ways."

"I am not wanton!" Autumn said indignantly.

"I guess Cracker thinks you are," Bish said, his dark brows knitted together in a scowl. "When he finds out that you're . . . that Agatha is . . . Uh-oh."

"Tell me about it," Autumn said. She plunked her elbow on the table and rested her chin in her hand. "He may never accept me as Autumn, nor forgive me for dusting off his precious Agatha. Even if I dress like a frump for the rest of my life, the fact remains that I'm really Autumn Stanton."

"Love conquers all!" Bish said.

"Like hell it does," Lisa said.

"Oh." Bish paused. "Well, anyone have a brilliant idea here?"

"Not really," Lisa said. "I think the only thing for

Autumn to do at this point is to proceed with her original plan of cooperating with Graham's transformation of Agatha. As she slowly changes into the image of Autumn, he may become more receptive to the fact that they're actually the same person."

"Wonderful," Autumn muttered.

"Sure would help a helluva lot if love conquered all," Bish said.

"Take a hike, Terzoni," Autumn said.

The next morning Graham poured himself a cup of coffee, then walked to Autumn's desk and sat down, groaning as he squeezed his temples. His head was killing him. Someone was beating a sledgehammer against his brain. He would never, he decided like the multitudes gone before, drink again!

He was definitely hung over. He was also mad as hell! Autumn Stanton was a witch. How dare she make a play for him! There she'd sat, agreeing to role-play as Agatha so she could hustle him. Where was her family loyalty? Poor Agatha. His sweet, innocent, trusting Agatha was at the mercy of that woman. Well, by damn, he was going to do something about this!

"Hello," Autumn sang out as she entered the office.

"Oh-h-h," Graham moaned, holding his head. "Not so loud, okay?"

"Is something wrong, Graham?"

"Little headache."

"Well, gee, I hope you didn't catch my cold."

"No, I'm sure I didn't. Agatha, I have to talk to you. Why don't you get a cup of coffee and come into my office."

"All right," she said. Oh, help, she thought frantically as she walked to the coffeepot. What was he going to say? He obviously wasn't in a terrific mood. His face was about the same shade as hers, due to the fact that she was wearing her olive-green suit again.

Carrying her mug, she walked into Graham's office and sat down in the chair in front of his desk. He had removed his jacket and tie, and had his head leaned back. She wanted to slither onto his lap, plant kisses all over his handsome, slightly off-color face, and make him forget his nasty hangover. She'd unbutton his shirt, sink her fingers into that yummy, curly hair on his chest, and—

"Ahem!" She cleared her throat loudly, shifting in her chair as desire swirled within her.

"Huh?" Graham said, lifting his head.

"You wished to speak to me, Graham?"

"Yes." He leaned forward and crossed his arms on the desk. "Agatha, I love you. I love you, and I'm having a nervous breakdown."

"I beg your pardon?"

"Love is proving to be a great deal more complicated than I'd anticipated."

"Do tell," she muttered into her mug.

"My mind is going in a dozen directions at once. I've got to slow down, regroup, take one thing at a time. I'm questioning my motives regarding certain areas of our relationship."

"I'm afraid I don't understand."

"I said I'd take you shopping for new clothes, remember? Well, why am I doing that?"

"I don't know. Why are you doing that? You said it was for my comfort."

"But maybe it isn't. I have to say this, Agatha, even at the risk of hurting your feelings. I may be trying to change your appearance because I can't handle your choice of clothes."

"That's okay," she said merrily. "Whatever turns you on, Graham."

"No, it's not okay!" he roared. She jumped and nearly spilled her coffee. "Oh-h-h, my head. Listen to me. You're like a butterfly that's still in its cocoon. You could emerge as a beautiful, delicate creature."

"Oh," she sighed. "What a sweet thing to say."

"Just listen!"

"Yes. Yes, of course. Carry on."

"See, one minute I feel that you have the right to realize the full potential of your beauty, and I could help you do that. Then, I don't want to because I hate the idea of other men looking at you. Then, *then*, comes the killer. I'm afraid that subconsciously I'm trying to change you to meet my standards, and that really stinks."

"It does?"

"Yes, dammit, it does!"

"Not if I'm willing to change for you. If we were in agreement on this, I really don't think there would be a problem."

"But Agatha, I said I loved you just the way you are!"

"New clothes aren't going to alter who I am on the inside, Graham. My outward appearance is of little importance to me. I won't toss away my values or outlooks for you, but I have no objection to redecorating the outer shell. The thing is, I'm not convinced you're sure how you want me to look."

"I know," he said, slouching back in his chair.

"Well, so far, you like my hair loose like this. How do you feel about these shoes of Autumn's?" She waved her foot in the air. "Mine are still in the trunk of your car."

"Don't mention that woman's name to me!"

"Autumn?" she said, all innocence. "Why shouldn't I speak of Autumn?"

He stood and walked over to her. He set her coffee mug on top of the desk, then sat down in the other chair and cradled her hand between his.

"Sweetheart," he said gently, "Autumn is not your best friend."

"She's my cousin."

"What I mean is, when she sees something she wants, she goes after it with no regard for other people's feelings."

"How can you say that? You don't even know her." She deserved an Academy Award for this performance, Autumn thought glumly. Now she had to sit here and listen to a dissertation on what a crumb-bum Autumn Stanton was. Brother!

"I met Autumn last night," Graham said.

"You did?" she asked, opening her eyes wide.

"I knew you were busy, so I got together with Bish to give him those plans. Autumn came into a bar with some woman named Leslie Wagner."

"Lisa. I . . . um, know Lisa Wagner."

"Oh. Well, anyway, Autumn made a play for me."

"What?" She gasped, then gasped again for good measure.

"I'm sorry. I know this is painful for you to hear. She even said she would be you, act like you or whatever, if I wanted her to. She's a fast worker all right. Really disgusting."

"Disgusting?" Autumn repeated, her voice squeaking. "Isn't that a bit harsh? Maybe you misunderstood what she—"

"No way. She was a Betty Bazooms at full tilt. I told her in no uncertain terms that I'm interested in you, then I walked out. She's not to be trusted, Agatha. It really bothers me that you're living with her. Look, I'll understand if you feel like crying. This is a heavy trip I've laid on you. Do you? Want to cry, I mean."

"No, thank you. Maybe later. Graham, this is all terribly confusing. I guess the part about Autumn being after your body is clear enough, but this business about my clothes is rather muddled. Are we going on a shopping trip or not?"

"Do you want to?"

"Only if you do."

"I do, but I don't know why I do! That's the part that's ripping me apart!"

"And I think you're placing far too much importance on your motives. It's the inner me that counts, Graham. I don't mind if you rearrange the frosting."

"It seems dishonest somehow."

"You had to say that word," she mumbled.

"Agatha, I guess I'll have to ask you to go along with me on this. I have to know the truth about myself. Then maybe I can get a handle on it and deal with it."

"That's a very reasonable request."

"In the meantime, I'm not going to make love to you."

"Why on earth not?"

"I can't! Who would I be making love to? The Agatha I claimed to love as you are, or the one I'm trying to change you into?"

"Who cares?" she said cheerfully.

"I do! Who is the new wardrobe for? You or me? Dammit, I don't know!"

"Oh. Well, let's get this show on the road, then. When can you go shopping?"

"Not until Saturday. I have to drive up to Fisher's property with him tomorrow."

"That's fine."

"Let's go out to dinner tonight, Agatha. We'll celebrate your finishing your internship. We won't discuss clothes or Autumn, we'll just relax and have a nice evening."

"I'd like that."

Graham stood and pulled her up into his arms, claiming her mouth in a kiss that was long and sensuous, and turned her knees to jelly.

Not make love to her? she thought. Oh, how absolutely, positively grim!

When he finally released her, she walked on trembling legs to the outer office and sank onto her chair. Things were so out of control it was ridiculous. It hadn't been very nice of Graham to call Autumn disgusting. Darn him and his honesty fetish. Now he was all strung out on why he wanted to shape up Agatha!

Well, she mused, she had to go along with the whole thing. Graham would transform Agatha into the image he wanted, and she would continually assure him his motives were fine and dandy, whatever they turned out to be. She also had a sneaky feeling she'd end up a carbon copy of Autumn. She'd seen Graham's reaction to Autumn in the bar. The man was not averse to beautiful women!

And then would come the critical turning point, the moment of truth. She would stand before Graham in her finery, be evidence that outer trappings do not change the inner being, and tell him the whole story, first page to last. She would declare her love for him, tell him that she, Autumn Stanton, loved him with every breath in her body. He'd either be thrilled to pieces, or he'd break her nose. She shook her head and sighed. How had she ever gotten herself into this mess? People on soap operas led calmer lives!

Graham squeezed the bridge of his nose and stared out the window at the fog covering San Francisco.

The cool gray city of love, he mused. There it all was. The cool, the gray, the city, and in his heart was the love. But what about Agatha? What was she feeling for him? She cared, he knew that, but did she love him? What would it do to her if he had to admit he had changed her appearance for himself? Would it hurt her so badly that he'd lose her? She claimed she didn't care, but how could she know until it happened? *If* it happened. Why didn't he know himself better than this? But, dammit, he wished she'd tell him that she loved him.

Seven

Sighing wistfully, Autumn viewed the vast array of lovely clothes in her closet. Wrapped in a fluffy towel, her hair a soft, fragrant cloud about her shoulders, her skin silken and glowing, she felt feminine and pretty. She sat on the edge of the bed and stared frowning at the extensive fashionable wardrobe.

How strange, she mused, that people placed so much emphasis on outer beauty. She was no exception. Before her was tangible evidence of time, money, and energy spent to assure that she owned the finest fashions available, so that she could look her best at all times. Matching shoes and purses, scarves and jewelry. No detail had been overlooked.

And she adored every bit of it.

She liked the way she felt about herself when she

had completed each ensemble and saw her reflection in the mirror. And she enjoyed the appreciative glances she received from men, the silent messages of approval.

It had been that way since the beginning of time, she supposed. Her studies in psychology had shown the human need to be accepted, loved, made to feel important and worthy. The world of business and free enterprise played on these emotions, shouting the news that certain clothes, hairstyles, makeup were the keys to gaining "beautiful people" status. "Thin was in," and extra pounds, gray hair, and wrinkles had to go. The masses listened and believed, and it became an ongoing competition.

Autumn had never questioned any of it until now. Until Graham, and Agatha, and the jumbled chaos she had created. It suddenly seemed ludicrous that all of her problems stemmed from material things like the clothes hanging in her closet.

Yet she could not ignore the yearning to reach among her favorite outfits and choose the perfect dress for her dinner date with Graham. She wanted to transform herself into a vision of loveliness and see Graham's appreciative gaze. She wanted heads to turn when they entered the restaurant and for people to whisper that they were such a striking couple.

Was it wrong? she wondered. Or was it normal to want approval from strangers as well as from the man she loved? Even more, if Graham decided he preferred her in Agatha's style of dress, would she really feel comfortable being less attractive than she knew she could be? How deep did her ego go?

Oh, darn it, what a mess she'd gotten herself into. And how disconcerting not to know herself better than this.

Autumn walked to the closet and tapped her fingertip against her chin as she considered the choices Agatha had for the evening. It was depressing at best, and she rolled her eyes. If only she could wear . . .

"Wait a minute," she said aloud. Why not nudge Graham along a bit? The poor man was in a terrible dilemma, raking himself over the coals about Agatha and the dos and don'ts of her transformation. She should help him any way she could. Agatha would be beautiful tonight and give Graham a show-and-tell demonstration of what the shopping trip could accomplish.

With a burst of excited energy, Autumn reached in the dresser for lacy underthings, then turned once again to the beckoning array in the closet.

The dress was sensational!

She floated it over her head and felt the soft black crepe glide into place. Scooped low over her breasts, it swept across her shoulders and dipped to her waist in back, displaying a healthy view of her ivory skin. A narrow sash nipped in her waist, then the skirt fell in soft folds to midcalf. She added thin-strapped black evening sandals, then applied her makeup to perfection. Her eyes were sparkling as she twirled in front of the mirror, smiling at her reflection.

Everything was going to be fine, she decided. She was Autumn Stanton, who was in love with Graham Kimble. Once he recovered from the shock of Agatha's appearance, she would tell him the truth of how the silly deception had come to be. She hated living in limbo, swallowing her declaration of love for Graham, playing a part that had gone on long enough.

Tonight was the night!

"Yes, it is," she said decisively. "Agatha shall fade into oblivion!"

Graham stepped into the elevator of Autumn's apartment building and nodded absently at the tall man who joined him. The stranger appeared to be in his late twenties and was wearing an air force uniform.

"Punch eight for me, will you?" the officer asked.

"That's where I'm going," Graham said as the doors swished closed.

"I hope my lovely friend is home," the officer said pleasantly. "I got an unexpected layover here, and didn't call her first."

"Well, good luck," Graham said, smiling.

"Yeah, I've really missed her."

The elevator bumped to a stop, the doors opened, and the officer motioned to Graham to precede him out of the car. They both turned to the right and started down the corridor. Graham slowed his step as he approached Autumn's door and saw out of the corner of his eye that the officer had done the same.

"I think we have a problem," the man said as they both halted in front of apartment eight fourteen. "I definitely should have called first."

"Not necessarily," Graham said. "Who are you here to see?"

The man frowned. "Autumn, of course. This is her apartment. Look, don't get uptight, buddy. I'll just say hello to her and be on my way."

"Don't worry about it," Graham said, knocking on the door. "Autumn is all yours."

"Huh?" The man looked totally confused.

Graham! Autumn thought when she heard the knock on the door. Oh, please, please understand!

She drew in a shaky breath, managed a weak smile, and opened the door. The smile slid off her chin and her mouth dropped open as she stared wide-eyed at the two handsome men before her. The next instant she slammed the door shut in their faces!

"Oh, good Lord!" she whispered, and yanked it open again. "Well, hi!" she said brightly. Her heart was racing, and a rushing noise filled her ears. She wanted to disappear into thin air. "Fancy meeting you two here," she added, attempting a smile that failed.

"Hi, sweetheart," the officer said. "May we come in?"

"What? Oh, of course." She stepped back. "Hello, Graham," she said, swallowing heavily as she shut the door.

"Autumn." He nodded slightly and definitely did not smile.

"Well," the other man said, "don't you have a hug for your—"

"Lover!" Autumn cried, flinging her arms around the officer's neck. "How are you? I've missed you. This is such a surprise!"

Graham cleared his throat. "Excuse me," he said, "but you two would obviously prefer to be alone. Would you just tell Agatha that I'm here?"

"Who?" the man asked.

"Agatha," Autumn said, and took a deep breath. "Yes, of course, Agatha. Well, she's running a bit late. She's still in the bathtub. I think we should all have a drink. Yes, that's a splendid idea. A drink."

"Maybe introductions are in order," the officer said. "Autumn, who is Agatha?"

"Her cousin," Graham said. "I'm Graham Kimble." He extended his hand.

"Cousin?" the man repeated, looking at Autumn as he absently shook Graham's hand.

"You've never met her," Autumn said. "Graham, this is Major Clint . . . Stanley. Clint, may I see you in the kitchen a moment, darling? Graham, do make yourself at home."

"What in the—" Clint began, but Autumn grabbed his arm and hauled him across the room.

"Hush, my love," she cooed. "Come into the kitchen where I can greet you properly."

In the kitchen, she collapsed against the counter, then slowly looked up to see Clint with his arms crossed over his chest and a deep frown on his face.

"I bet you wonder what's going on here, don't you?" she said.

"I'm a tad curious," he agreed, nodding. "What have you gotten yourself into this time, Autumn? Last time I checked my ID I was Clint Stanton. And I'm your brother, not your lover. Who in the hell is Agatha? We don't have a cousin named Agatha."

"Keep your voice down. Graham mustn't find out

the truth this way, Clint, or he'll figure you forced me into telling him. I was going to explain everything to him tonight, but he'd never believe that now."

Clint chuckled and shook his head. "I have a feeling this one is a beaut. Okay, let's have it. Spill the beans."

In a hushed voice, Autumn rushed through the story of how Agatha came to exist, Autumn's love for Graham, and the subsequent complicated state of affairs. Clint whistled low and long when she came to a breathless halt.

"You're amazing," he said. "You really are." He reached into a cupboard for glasses. "Graham is going to think we're really into something hot and heavy out here," he said, laughing softly. "We'd better make an appearance with those drinks you promised. I swear, Autumn, you need a keeper. The part that really blows my mind is that my baby sister is in love. I'm going back in there and check this guy out."

"He can't stand me," she said miserably. "He's in love with Agatha. Clint, please be careful while you're talking to Graham. He mustn't suspect that—"

"Trust me," he said, kissing her on the end of her nose. "I won't blow your cover. But kiddo, you're in trouble. The longer you keep up this charade, the harder it's going to be to dig your way out. No guy likes to be conned, especially a man in love."

"I know that! But don't you understand why I can't tell him tonight?"

"Yeah, I suppose. It would look like I forced your

hand. I'll follow your lead, but I sure hope you know what we're doing."

"Don't count on it," she mumbled, leaving the kitchen. "Here's the drink I promised you, Graham," she sang out as she reentered the living room.

Graham turned slowly from where he was staring at the books on the bookshelf, and frowned.

Damn, he thought, it threw him every time he looked at Autumn. Everything about her was a duplicate of Agatha; her voice, the way she gestured with her hands, everything. And that dress! Autumn was a beautiful, beautiful woman. Agatha could be transformed into that kind of picture of loveliness if she wore the right clothes. He'd be the envy of every guy who saw her on his arm. She was just so damn pretty! A knot had tightened in his gut when Autumn had plastered herself to that fly boy. It was like watching Agatha in the arms of another man! What in the hell had they been doing out in that kitchen? No, it didn't matter because this was Autumn, not Agatha. Lord, he was going to blow a fuse in his brain!

"Graham?" Autumn said. "Clint has your drink."

"What? Oh, thanks." He accepted the glass.

Autumn's gaze flickered over Graham's steel-gray suit, and she decided he was the most handsome man in San Francisco. As her gaze swept upward, she found herself looking into the dark pools of his eyes, and her pulse quickened. Neither of them moved. They simply stared at each other.

"About Agatha," Graham said finally, taking a

swallow of his drink. "Do you think she's about ready?"

"Who? Oh! I'll go check," Autumn said, and hurried into the bedroom.

Dammit, Graham silently fumed, she'd gotten to him! Another two seconds and he'd have hauled her into his arms and kissed her! She made the blood run hot in his veins and—

"Autumn tells me you're an architect," Clint said, sinking onto the sofa.

"Yeah. Have you known Autumn long?"

"Years and years. Great gal. Smart as a whip, too. Not often a man finds such a rare combination of beauty and brains. I envy the guy who marries her."

"That's not you?"

"Me? No. No, I don't plan on marrying Autumn."

"Because," Autumn said, coming back into the room, "I'm in love with someone else. Very, very deeply in love with someone else."

"The lucky bugger," Clint said. "Wouldn't you feel fortunate to have a woman like Autumn in love with you, Graham?"

"Sure I would. Is Agatha ready?"

"Not quite," Autumn said. "Graham, about what happened in the bar last night. You totally misinterpreted what I was saying. I'm afraid you got an impression of me that isn't true."

"Oh?" he said.

"I wasn't trying to make a play for you. As I told you, I'm in love."

"Then how do you explain Clint being here? Forget it. It's none of my business."

"Oh, Autumn and I are just friends," Clint said.

"I view her as I would my own sister. No, sir, when this little gal says she's in love, she means it. She's a straight arrow. Even if she did something that appeared fishy, it wouldn't be because she takes love lightly. Right, Autumn? Right. The man who loved her should be willing in return to hear her out before passing any judgment. He should listen to the whole story."

"Clint—" Autumn started.

"The story she should explain immediately," he interrupted, staring hard at her, "because love is the big leagues, and people are going to be hurt if she doesn't."

"Are you sure you don't want to be alone?" Graham asked. "You sound like you're speaking in a secret code."

"Give us five minutes," Clint said, getting to his feet. "Go into the kitchen, Autumn."

"But—"

"Now!"

"Weird group," Graham muttered, and drained his glass.

In the kitchen, Autumn planted her hands on her hips and glared at her brother.

"What are you doing?" she whispered. "You promised me you'd go along with this whole thing."

"That was before I took a good look at Kimble. Dammit, Autumn, you're ripping the guy up! He comes unglued every time he's close to you because he's in love with you, but doesn't know he is or . . . whatever. The point is, how do you think he feels realizing he's attracted to you while his true love is in the bathtub in the other room? This is cold, really rotten. You've got to tell him the truth tonight, just like you planned."

"Tonight? Now? Oh, Clint, no!"

"Yes! You're putting that guy through the wringer, and it's not fair. I just hope that . . . well . . ."

"That what?"

"It's not too late. I wouldn't even want to bet how he's going to react."

"Oh, dear."

"March, little sister. It's time to face the music."

"I can't. My stomach hurts. I think I'm going to throw up."

"That one works on Dad, not me," Clint said. "Go! No, wait a minute."

"Oh, thank goodness." She leaned back against the counter.

"Look, I think Graham's a decent guy, but I'm also your brother. I'm not leaving you here alone in what could turn into a war zone. Kimble could become very upset."

"Clint, for heaven's sake, he isn't going to murder me. I know Graham. I love Graham! Listen to me, Clint. This is not the night for me to tell him."

"That part is not up for discussion. We men have to stick together as protection against screwy women."

"Well, I never!" She folded her arms across her chest. "That was rude. You make me sound like a bubblehead."

"There are times, sweet Autumn, when you qualify, and this is one of them. I can't believe the mess you've made of this whole thing. Well, it's getting straightened out. Right now!"

"Oh, dear," Autumn said, following him from the kitchen.

"How about another drink, Graham?" Clint asked, back in the living room.

"No, thanks. Autumn, don't you think Agatha is ready by now? I made reservations for dinner."

"Autumn would like to speak with you privately," Clint said. "I'll just go into the bedroom and make myself scarce."

"Hold it just a damn minute," Graham said. "You're not going in that bedroom. Agatha's getting dressed in there!"

"Oh, Lord," Clint said.

Autumn ran her tongue nervously over her bottom lip as she stared at Graham. This was it, she thought frantically. The turning point of her life had come. The moment of truth. All her eggs in one basket. If she could think of some more great old sayings, she could postpone this nightmare!

"Au-tumn!" Clint growled.

"Yes!" she said, taking a deep breath.

"I'll go in the bedroom," Clint repeated, starting across the room.

"One more step, fly boy," Graham said none too quietly, "and I'm going to take you apart!"

"Dammit, Autumn!" Clint said. "Talk to this man. He's about to break my face!"

"You always told me you were so tough," she said, and sniffed indignantly.

"Not against guys put together like he is! I know my limits. Tell him that Agatha isn't in the damn bedroom!"

"Agatha isn't in the damn bedroom," she said in a small voice.

"Thank you," Clint said, and beat a hasty exit.

"What?" Graham asked.

"He said, 'Thank you,' " Autumn said, smiling weakly.

"Agatha isn't in there?" he roared. "Then where in the hell is she? Has something happened to her?"

"No! No, of course not. Graham, we have to talk. Just stay calm, okay? There is a perfectly reasonable explanation for all of this. In fact, it's really quite humorous when you stop to think about it. Oh, my, yes, a very funny chain of events."

"Where in the hell is Agatha?"

She cringed. "Wouldn't you like to sit down?" she asked.

"No!"

"Oh. Well, then I guess it's time for me to explain what's going on, isn't it? Yes, it certainly is."

"Autumn," Graham said through clenched teeth, "I demand to know where Agatha is. And don't tell me she went down the drain in the bathtub!"

"Agatha," Autumn said, taking another deep breath, "as you know her, isn't here, because she . . . I decided to surprise you and wear this dress for our dinner date. Then when Clint arrived . . ."

"You're Agatha?" Graham asked, his eyes widening with disbelief.

"Yes. Well, no, not exactly."

"Dammit, quit messing around!"

"Graham, Agatha doesn't exist! She's never existed. It was always me, Autumn Stanton, you were talking to and . . . stuff. I was gathering data for my thesis, you see, and I created Agatha to help prove my theory. But then I—"

"What did you say?" he interrupted, his voice a hoarse whisper. "What?"

"It was all supposed to be so simple," she said, throwing up her hands, "but everything went wrong. Or very right, depending on how you look at it. Oh, Graham, I never meant to deceive you! I was going to tell you the whole story, I swear it. But I didn't want to lose—"

"Damn you!" he yelled, yanking the knot of his tie loose. "All you've been doing is gathering data? I'm nothing more than a—a white mouse in a laboratory to you?"

"No!"

"Good Lord, you even let me make love to you! You really give your research your all, don't you?"

Clint flung open the bedroom door. "You slept with my sister?" he shouted. "You're dead meat, Kimble!"

"Clint, go away!" Autumn said.

"Sister? Agatha . . . Autumn is your sister?"

"Damn right she is!"

"Clint, go to your room!" Autumn ordered.

"You never said you'd gone to bed with the guy, Autumn," Clint said. "What in the hell did you think you were doing?"

"Gathering data!" Graham snapped. "Your charming sister is a cold-hearted con artist."

"I am not!"

"Did you get a good laugh out of this, Autumn?" Graham asked bitterly. "How did you keep a straight face when I told Agatha that I loved her?"

"Oh, Graham, please," Autumn said, her eyes filling with tears.

"I did, you know," he said, his voice suddenly low. "Love her. I thought she was everything I had ever wanted in a woman, a wife, the mother of my children. Then I felt maybe I wasn't being fair by not giving her the chance to discover how beautiful she was. But then you know all this, don't you, because I bared my soul to you."

"Oh, Graham," Autumn said, tears spilling onto her cheeks, "listen to me, let me explain. Please, Graham, there's so much I have to tell you. It's not what you're thinking. I wasn't playing games with you. I love you! I was willing to be whomever you wanted me to be to prove that love."

"Spare me," he said, starting toward the door. "I've had enough of this. You can deck me if you want to, Clint, but you should remember I made love to Agatha, and she doesn't even exist."

"Yeah," Clint said quietly, shoving his hands into his pockets. "Forget I mentioned it."

"Graham, wait!" Autumn cried, a sob catching in her throat.

He stopped by the door and turned to look at her. A flicker of pain crossed his face, settling into the dark depths of his eyes. Then he clenched his jaw and squared his shoulders.

"Good-bye, Agatha," he said, "and Autumn, and whoever else you are when the mood strikes. If things don't pan out for your doctorate, you can always be an actress. You sure had me fooled."

"Oh, Graham, please don't do this. I love you!"

"You don't know what the word means," he said,

then left the apartment, slamming the door behind him.

"Graham!"

"Damn," Clint said. He hurried to Autumn and gathered her into his arms as she sobbed uncontrollably. "What a helluva mess. I've never seen a guy so torn up. And you're in no better shape. You really love him, don't you?"

"Oh, yes, Clint, I do. I never meant to hurt him. He'll never forgive me. He loved Agatha, and it's my fault he doesn't have her anymore. What Graham doesn't realize is that the only difference between Agatha and me is the way we dressed. Our values, outlooks, everything else is the same! I was even willing to be frumpy if he wanted me to. I think he was changing his mind about that, though. Oh, Clint, I'm so unhappy. I've lost the only man I've ever loved!"

"Hey," he said, gripping her by the shoulders and moving her away from him. "You're giving up? My sister, the scrapper, who once spent an entire night in a tree because Mom wouldn't let her bleach her hair blond, is giving up? I'm surprised at you, Autumn."

"Graham hates me!"

"Wrong. Graham loves you."

"No, he doesn't! He loves Agatha!"

"Good Lord, you're dense. You just said the only difference between you and Agatha was your clothes. He fell in love with the person, the inner being, too, you know, and that's you. Oh, he loves you, Autumn. He just doesn't realize it at the moment. He's hurt, and mad as hell."

"Graham thinks I'm a cold-hearted creature with

no feelings, who was doing nothing more than collecting data for my thesis. He's probably convinced I took notes when we— Forget it."

"I'm trying to. It's hard for me to come to grips with the fact that my baby sister is all grown up. But you are, and you're in love. You've got to calm down, regroup, and plan a new attack. If you quit now, I'll smack your butt."

"That's what Dad did when I finally came down out of the tree," she said, flopping onto the sofa. "Wait until Graham tells Bish about this. Bish will probably pretend he's a hitman and buy me some cement boots."

"Bish Terzoni?"

"Yes, he's Graham's best friend. Do you know him?"

"Sure do. Bish and I played football together in college. Hey, does he call Graham Cracker?"

"Yes."

"I remember him telling stories about his escapades with his buddy Cracker. They'd planned on going to the same college, even though Bish was a little older than Graham; then Bish got a football scholarship to Stanford. Dad does some big business with Bish these days."

"Bish recognized me right off when I was Agatha. He'd seen pictures of me at the house and knew who I was. I convinced him not to tell Graham that I was Autumn. Bish is going to murder me for hurting Graham."

"Maybe not. He'd want to see Graham happy, wouldn't he? Bish is a nice guy. Maybe, just maybe, he'd be willing to help you."

"Help me take a long walk off a short pier, no

doubt. Oh-h-h, I'm going to cry for the next ten years straight."

"You don't have time for that. You have to plan your strategy."

"Do you always have to talk so military?"

"Gets the job done, doesn't it? Go put on some jeans, and I'll take you out for pizza. I'm hungry."

"How can you think of food at a time like this?" she wailed. "My heart is broken!"

"And my stomach is empty. Change your clothes."

"All right," she said, sighing deeply. "I chose this dress especially for Graham and our dinner date."

"Believe me, sweetheart, he noticed it. Graham Kimble is very aware of the fact that Autumn Stanton is a beautiful woman."

"But he loves Agatha!" she said, walking into the bedroom.

"So do something about it!" Clint yelled after her.

Graham entered his apartment and tossed his jacket onto a chair. He stared at it for a long moment, remembering the time he had snatched a jacket back up because a wife wouldn't want to live with a slob.

"Ah, hell!" he muttered, and strode to the small bar. He started to pour himself a stiff drink, then decided not to. Autumn had done enough damage. She wasn't going to turn him into a boozer, too. Damn her. Damn that Autumn Stanton and her lies. It had all been a sick game to her. All of it. And

Agatha was gone. The woman he loved had vanished, had never even really existed.

He missed her already, Graham realized as he sat down on the sofa. He missed his Agatha, with her big green eyes and silky hair, her ivory skin, and her lilting laughter. Lord, she'd looked sensational in that dress tonight. No, wait. That wasn't Agatha, that had been Autumn. No, that was Agatha, who had changed her appearance especially for him as a surprise. And oh, man, talk about a fantastic surprise! Agatha had— No, dammit, there was no such person as Agatha Stanton!

"I'm cracking up," he said to a pillow at the end of the sofa. "This is it. The last grain of sand is sifting out of my bucket!" There was also, he thought miserably, a knife twisted in his gut. Autumn's deception had hurt so damn much. He thought he'd found his future in Agatha, and it was all a lie. He felt empty, drained, and lonely as hell.

So, now what? he asked himself. Back to the Betty Bazooms and the fast lane, he supposed, though the thought of it held no appeal. He wanted to make love to Agatha. Who was Autumn. "Oh, Lord have mercy," he said, sitting upright. "I made love to Autumn Stanton!" And it had been the most incredible experience of his life. Emotions had been interwoven with the physical act, and a lump had actually formed in his throat. Their joining had been a celebration, a coming together like none he had ever known. There had been so much passion, sharing, an equal giving and taking. It had been a merging of hearts and souls, as well as bodies. And it had taken place with Autumn.

Graham ran his hand down his face, then pulled his shirt loose from his pants and unbuttoned it. He leaned his head back on top of the sofa and closed his eyes, only to see visions of both Agatha and Autumn. Back and forth they floated, interchanging one into the other, until a painful cadence beat against his temples.

"Damn," he muttered. He walked to the bar. And tossed back a shot of Scotch, then coughed as it burned his throat. He wandered into the kitchen, pulled open the refrigerator door, then slammed it shut. "Damn," he said again.

Back in the living room, he stared out the window at the breathtaking view of San Francisco. He replayed in his mind once more the lovemaking he had shared with Autumn, and heat surged through his body. The questions pounded against his brain, demanding answers.

Why in heaven's name couldn't he dismiss the memory of Autumn's softness, her passion, as she lay beneath him? It had all been a hoax, a charade, so why did their lovemaking still hold such meaning for him? Even now, knowing he had not been with his beloved Agatha, their union touched his emotions and ignited his desire. It had been nothing more than a one-night stand to Autumn to gather her damnable data. So why couldn't he just forget it ever happened, chalk it up as one more score? He detested Autumn Stanton, and he burned with the need to bury himself deep within her honeyed warmth again. What in the hell was that woman doing to him?

"Get out of my head, Autumn Stanton," he said to the night. "Haven't you done enough to me for one lifetime?" She'd even told him that she loved him! The words he'd been hoping, praying, to hear Agatha speak had been delivered by Autumn . . . while she'd been crying . . . while tears had been streaming down her face. Lord, she'd looked sad, sounded sad, as though her heart were breaking in two, just as his was.

"Forget it," he said, shaking his head. "She could moonlight as an actress, for cripe's sake. I never intend to see her again! Ever. Hell, I'm going to bed!"

But Graham did see Autumn again. Through the long, dark hours of the night she crept into his restless slumber, haunting his dreams. She was wearing the beautiful black dress, her hair was a tumbled cascade of strawberry-blond waves, and she was crying.

Eight

The next morning, Autumn paced back and forth across her living room. She was wearing her scruffy terry-cloth robe and a frown. While she was relieved that the long night, which she'd spent tossing and turning, was over, the dawn seemed to emphasize the hopelessness of her situation.

She loved Graham. She missed him. She wanted to tell herself that everything was his fault so she could be furious with him, but she couldn't. There was only one villain in the scenario, and that was she. There was no one to blame but herself for the ache in her heart and the pain she had seen in Graham's fudge-dark eyes.

Clint had been so dear, she mused as she continued to pace. He had stuffed her full of pizza and encouraging words before bringing her back to the apartment. He'd hugged her tightly, told her to fight like hell for Graham Kimble, then left her to catch his plane. Left her alone and lonely, and she'd cried. Lord, had she ever cried! But her tears had accomplished nothing more than to give her a roaring headache, puffy eyes, and a red nose.

And now, in the light of the new day, Autumn was faced with yet another dilemma: the promise she had made to her aunt Nancy. Graham had to have a secretary, and Autumn had taken on the job. She had given her word to her aunt that she would work hard for Graham, that his office would be run efficiently in Nancy's absence. She'd also sworn that no harm would come to darling Graham because of her charade. Well, so much for that part. She'd managed to smash Graham's heart to smithereens.

"I can't go to his office," she mumbled. "He'll throw me out on my gorgeous tush." Surely he'd get a temporary secretary. But what if she was a ding-dong who flubbed everything up? Graham was so busy, he didn't have time for incompetence. There was no choice in the matter. She would offer to stay until Aunt Nancy returned, Graham would refuse to have her there, and she'd leave. But maybe her conscience would be eased a bit for breaking her promise to her aunt.

She dressed in a teal-blue silk shirtwaist, carefully applied her makeup, and brushed her hair until it shone. Her reflection in the mirror told her she looked lovely. The ache in her heart reaffirmed how miserable she felt. After one more wobbly sigh, she picked up her purse and left the apartment.

*   *   *

"Dammit!" Graham muttered, solidly hitting the typewriter. "Considering what I paid for this thing, you'd think it could spell!" As the office door opened behind him, he spun around in the chair. "Autumn," he said. "What are you doing here?" Dear heaven, he thought, look at her! She was beautiful. Absolutely beautiful. Oh, hell, who cared! "Well?" he said, glaring at her.

Autumn closed the door, then determinedly lifted her chin. Graham was tired, she thought. He looked so worn out. She wanted to hold him, comfort him, declare her love, gaze into his eyes forever, just like in romance novels.

"Graham," she said, immediately aware that her voice was unsteady, "I know you don't want to see me, but I felt I had to come to offer my services as your secretary. I promised my aunt Nancy that your office would run efficiently in her absence."

"Nancy is your aunt?" he said, getting to his feet. "Brother, a person can't trust anyone these days."

"Please don't blame her for this. I convinced her to let me take her place."

"Ahh, yes, Autumn the actress. Nancy didn't stand a chance."

"Did you call a temporary placement service?"

"I'm not in the mood to train someone. I planned on doing this junk myself. So far, I've discovered I can't type worth a damn."

"Graham, look, I realize this is an uncomfortable situation at best, but we're both adults. I'm a good secretary, and you know it. You won't have to communicate with me other than to tell me what you want done. There's no reason for your productivity to suffer because of my mistake in judgment."

"Mistake in judgment?" he repeated. "Is that what you call the shambles you've made of my life? A tiny little mistake in judgment? I've got a newsflash for you, Autumn Stanton. You're a walking demolition derby!"

"Oh, is that so!" she snapped. "Well, for your information, I don't feel that terrific myself, Mr. Kimble. In the middle of this chaotic mess, I fell in love with you! I do recall mentioning that fact to you last night. How do you think it feels to be in love with a man who loves another woman? Especially when that woman doesn't exist!"

"Don't say those words," he said, brushing past her. "Don't you dare say that you love me! I don't know what you're up to this time, but it isn't going to work. You're as phony as a three-dollar bill. I really don't want you here, Autumn, but I have my business to think of. Sit down there and type, but don't speak to me!"

"Fine. Dandy. Great," she said, plopping onto the chair. "I have nothing further to say to you, anyway. Except, you can fix your own damn coffee!"

"Hell," he muttered, and stalked into his office.

Autumn stuck her tongue out at his broad back. "Rude," she said to the typewriter. "He's a very rude man. And I love him so much."

Damn her, Graham silently fumed as he stared unseeing out the window. Damn that Autumn. He'd spent a hellish night with her in his dreams, then she showed up in his office! Showed up looking like she'd stepped out of *Vogue*, and telling him she loved him. Why was she doing this, declaring her love for him? It didn't make sense. None of what had transpired between them had really meant anything to her beyond her damnable research. He should dust her off, forget her, and he would if she didn't look so much like Agatha! The Agatha he had imagined creating when he took her shopping.

"I never accepted Agatha as she was," he said softly as a knot tightened in his stomach. He had been hellbent on changing her. He would have done it, transformed Agatha into Autumn, into a striking, beautiful woman. Then he would have had it all his way; an intelligent Harriet Housewife to raise his children, and a gorgeous, passionate woman to share his bed. Because oh, yes, Agatha had been passionate, so giving when he'd taken her into his arms.

"Oh, Lord," he mumbled, running his hand over the back of his neck. There he went again. That was Autumn he'd made love to! Autumn! Dammit, he had to get a handle on this before he ended up getting shipped to the farm. Agatha was gone. There had never been an Agatha. He had to accept that. But it wasn't that easy to do when a carbon copy of her was sitting in his outer office! But Autumn was a conniving con artist, with no conscience or regard for the feelings of others. He really didn't like that woman!

He stared up at the ceiling as he sifted things through his mind. Autumn owed him, he decided. The ache in his heart and the teetering state of his sanity were her doing. Well, she could just pay up!

He spun on his heel and strode out to Autumn's desk. He planted his hands flat on the surface and leaned forward until his nose was about an inch from hers and he was looking directly into her big green eyes.

"Listen up, Ms. Stanton," he said, a muscle twitching in his jaw. "You've turned me inside out and hung me out to dry. I'm losing my mind and it's all your fault. The only way I can completely forget Agatha is to rid myself of you! When you go, so does she. I need to reaffirm that you are not remotely close to what I want in a woman. Therefore, we are going to spend as much time together as necessary until I accomplish what I need to, to regain control of my life!"

"But—"

"You owe me, Autumn Stanton, and I'm collecting. And I swear, if you play your sick game with me and say that you love me, I'll break your big toe. Got that?"

"But—"

"I'll pick you up at seven tonight. Pack a suitcase."

"What?" she shrieked.

"You heard me! We're going to my cabin for the weekend. I'm getting you and Agatha out of my system once and for all, and I don't intend to waste any more time than necessary doing it!"

"And if I refuse to go with you?"

"Then you can kiss your aunt Nancy's job goodbye, because I'll fire her!"

"That's blackmail!"

"Damn right it is, lady. I can play just as dirty as you can. Well?"

"I withdraw every nice thing I ever said about you, Graham Kimble!"

"Seven o'clock!"

"I'll be ready!"

"Good!" He stomped back into his office.

Autumn blinked once slowly to see if she'd wake up. Oh, dear, it hadn't been a nightmare, it was real! She was going away with Graham for the weekend. The man was a lunatic! He was going to forget Agatha by spending time with Autumn? That was dumb, made no sense at all. On the other hand, maybe it did. Graham was physically attracted to her. It was apparent every time his gaze swept over her, missing no detail of her figure. He did not, however, care for her as a person, no doubt believing her values were far removed from those of his wonderful Agatha. So, his dislike of her would override his attraction, and that would be that.

Wrong, she thought, smiling brightly. What Mr. Graham Cracker didn't know was that she, in essence, was Agatha! She wanted to be a wife and mother, tend to her family's needs. She'd have a small psychology practice as her personal outlet and help create a warm, loving home. The vows she spoke when she married would be sacred, held in reverence until the day she died. She wanted all of those things. And she wanted Graham.

With a decisive nod she rolled a piece of paper into the typewriter and began to type. A few minutes later the office door opened and Bish Terzoni entered.

"Good morning, Aga—Autumn?" He stopped dead in his tracks.

"Hello, hello," she sang out.

"What are you doing here? What's going on? Why are you Autumn? Where's Cracker?"

She frowned. "Which one of those should I answer first? Why don't you go talk to Graham, and let him bring you up to date."

"What kind of mood is he in?"

"Don't ask."

"Uh-oh." Bish strode across the room, entered Graham's office, and closed the door behind him. Autumn folded her hands on the top of the desk and waited, picturing in her mind the scene being played out in the other room.

"Any second now," she said finally.

"You're going to do what?" Bish bellowed. "Dammit, Cracker, have you flipped your switch?"

Autumn laughed and resumed her typing.

In Graham's office, Bish raked his hand through his thick dark hair and scowled at Graham.

"It's the only way," Graham said. "I can't take any more of this. I look at Autumn, I see Agatha. I tell myself there is no Agatha, then there she is smiling at me, gazing at me with her beautiful green eyes. I want to kiss her, hold her, but it isn't her, it's Autumn!"

"So, kiss the living daylights out of Autumn!"

"No! Autumn is a shallow, self-centered, out-for-herself woman. She used me for her damn research with no regard for my emotional well-being. I despise that woman."

"So why are you kidnapping her and dragging her off to the cabin for the weekend? That's crazy!"

"No, it's not," Graham said, beginning to pace the floor. "I took Agatha to Fisher's property in

Marin County. We walked through the woods, shared the peaceful setting. It was great. Well, at least until it started to rain. Even then Agatha was terrific about getting soaked, a really good sport. I was imagining what it would be like to take her to my cabin, just the two of us."

"So?"

"So, Autumn will hate it. The flash-and-dash types I've known don't want any part of getting back to nature. Their idea of roughing it is a weekend without a hot tub. I'm going to do a shock treatment on myself, show myself once and for all that there is no Agatha, then be finished with this nightmare."

"I see," Bish said thoughtfully.

"And don't try to lay a guilt trip on me for dragging Autumn up there. She owes me, Bish. What she did to me was really lousy."

"What if your plan doesn't work?"

"It'll work. Autumn will detest a weekend in the woods. Agatha would have loved it, I just know she would have. I'll have no choice but to face the truth, then I can get on with my life. As it stands, my brain is mush."

"But Cracker, you've got a slick cabin up there, all the comforts of home. True, there's no hot tub, but there's a microwave, a stereo system, a freezer full of food, fine wine in the pantry. You call that roughing it?"

"Things could get a little sticky if the electricity didn't work."

"You wouldn't."

"Damn right I would!"

"You're cold, Cracker."

"I'm desperate! I've got to get Agatha out of my system! Everything is jumbled together in my brain. I relive memories of Agatha, then realize it was really Autumn. My mind is made up. I'm taking her there, and by the time the weekend is over I'll be a free man again. It's the only way."

"Very interesting," Bish said slowly, nodding his head. "A bit drastic, but interesting. Well, good luck."

"That's it? Don't you want another half hour or so to try to talk me out of it?"

Bish placed his hand on Graham's shoulder. "Nope," he said. "Go for it, buddy. Yes, sir, just do your thing. Get Agatha Stanton out of your life once and for all. It's my fervent hope that you'll see Autumn for exactly what she is."

"No doubt about it," Graham said rather smugly. "Actually, this plan is borderline genius."

"Absolutely," Bish said, suppressing a smile. "Well, I've got to shove off. I'll talk to you on Monday and get a full report."

"I'll buy you a steak to celebrate the reclaiming of my sanity."

"You're on. See ya, Cracker."

"Bish, are you ever going to stop calling me that?"

Bish laughed and left the office. As he passed Autumn's desk, he grinned, winked, and gave her a thumbs-up sign. Autumn smiled in delight.

The remainder of the morning was quiet. Very quiet. Graham emerged from his office only long enough to bark orders at Autumn, and each time she replied with a crisp, "Yes, sir." He glared, she frowned. And neither made the coffee. At noon

Graham said he was leaving to meet Fisher and would pick Autumn up at seven sharp. She informed him in a cool tone that she would be ready.

And she was. Dressed in jeans, a bulky fisherman's sweater, and tennis shoes, she set her suitcase and heavy jacket by the door just before seven. Cricket had been tucked away with a neighbor who adored the cat, the plants had been watered. Everything was under control . . . except Autumn's nerves.

The angry tension that had emanated from Graham through the entire day had taken its toll on her, and she was exhausted. She was also well aware that her future happiness hinged on the outcome of this weekend. What Graham viewed as a means of ridding himself of Agatha and Autumn, she saw as her only hope of convincing him that they belonged together forever.

She also knew that the ensuing hours would call for total honesty on her part. Oh, she'd phonied up on occasional dates in the past in the name of kindness. She'd suffered through endless hockey games when she'd been seeing one of the players, and had yawned her way through poetry readings when she'd been briefly intrigued with a bearded writer.

But with Graham, everything was different. Their relationship had begun under a cloud of deception, and there would be no more of it. She would be herself, Autumn Stanton, and pray that Cupid was on her side. It would help immensely, she thought, if Cupid were an avid reader of romance novels.

At seven o'clock on the dot, Graham arrived. Dressed in tight jeans and a burgundy sweater, he seemed to fill the room with his presence. Autumn couldn't keep her gaze from roaming up and down his magnificent body, and her heart went into overdrive.

"Ready?" he asked gruffly, not looking directly at her.

"Yes."

"What about the cat?"

"Cricket is at a neighbor's."

"Fine." He picked up her jacket and suitcase. "Let's go."

"I can carry those."

"Get the lights and the door," he said sharply. "We're wasting time."

"Brother," she muttered, then did as she was instructed and followed him out of the apartment.

The night was chilly and damp, and the mist hanging low over the city created an almost eerie atmosphere. Graham drove the Ferrari through the city, then onto the Golden Gate Bridge. Memories of their previous trip across the bridge assaulted Autumn. She had been Agatha on the day they'd gone to Fisher's property, chattering away about the history of the bridge. She had laughed with Graham, shared with him, and later made love with him. It had been a day of wondrous joy and discovery, of the giving of her heart as well as her body. It had been heaven.

And now? she wondered. The silence in the car was oppressive. The same tension she had sensed earlier in Graham was nearly palpable in the small enclosure. His jaw was tightly clenched, and he was gripping the steering wheel with more force than necessary. What they'd had together, she had destroyed, and the realization of that brought an ache to her heart and a sigh from her lips.

"Cold?" Graham asked.

"No. I'll put my jacket on if I get any chillier. Graham, you wouldn't really have fired my aunt Nancy, would you?"

"No, of course not. I couldn't run that office without her. And besides, I like her. She's a very nice lady."

"She adores you. She's so proud of what you've accomplished in your career. I think she sees you as another one of her sons."

"You have a large family, right? Not just one cousin."

"A very large family, and they're wonderful. My parents are on vacation at the moment. Everyone gathers at their home for the holidays, and it's marvelous chaos. Clint is always showing up with some of his air force chums in tow, and my mother just sets some more places at the table. Nothing fazes my folks. Of course, raising me and Clint required that they be ready for anything."

"You were a handful, huh?" he said, glancing over at her.

She laughed. "Unbelievable. Oh, the scraps we got into and the pranks we pulled were grim. My father says it will serve me right if my children have the same temperament. He loves to say, 'Then you'll pay the piper, my girl.' Clint says he's never getting married and running that risk."

"I don't see you as the marrying type, either," Graham said tersely.

"On the contrary. That day in your office when I . . . when Agatha was explaining how she felt about balancing a family and career, those were my sentiments."

"Come on, Autumn," he said with a snort of disgust, "give me a break. I have built-in radar for women who play hard and fast, and you're one of them. Don't give me this hearth-and-home, babies-and-husband bit, because it won't wash. I'm not denying that you have more intelligence than the average Betty Bazooms, but other than that, you're popped out of the same mold."

"You're wrong, Graham," she said softly.

"The hell I am," he said, his voice low and fervent.

Autumn turned her head to hide the sudden tears that had sprung to her eyes. Icy misery had washed over her when she'd heard the bitterness in Graham's voice, the scorn. Was it hopeless? she wondered. Graham was so hurt and so mistrusting of everything she said and did. Did she stand any chance at all of breaking through the walls he'd built around himself? How was she ever going to convince him to believe in her, believe that she loved him with every fiber of her being? Had she lost the battle before it really even began? Had she lost her Graham?

The uncomfortable silence fell again as Graham turned off the main thoroughfare and headed farther into Marin County, in the opposite direction from the way they had gone to Fisher's property. Autumn wondered absently how long the drive to the cabin would take, then decided she really didn't care. With a weary sigh, she leaned her head back and closed her eyes. A few minutes later, she drifted off to sleep.

Graham glanced over at her and frowned. Autumn must consider him a gullible idiot, he thought. Did she really expect him to buy that bull about her wanting a family in addition to her career? Why didn't she just give it a rest, knock off the phony garbage? There was nothing to accomplish by her rattling off that spiel, because he was wise to her now.

But he'd have to stay on his toes, he realized. When she'd been talking about her family, he'd started to relax, had enjoyed hearing about her clan, and the devilish little girl she'd been. And she had laughed. Lord, he loved that sound. He'd also be kidding himself if he said he hadn't noticed how she looked in her jeans and sweater. They molded her body to perfection—and he knew every inch of that lovely body. Every soft, satiny inch. He had only to gaze at her to remember the feel of her skin next to his, the lush fullness of her breasts, the—

"Damn," he muttered, shifting almost guiltily as heat shot through him. Well, he would just ignore the physical effect Autumn had on him, because he had no intention of sleeping with that woman again. Ever!

With a firm nod of his head, Graham pressed harder on the gas pedal and the powerful vehicle shot forward. They would arrive at the cabin about ten o'clock, he calculated, and that would mark the beginning of his all-out campaign. By the end of the weekend he would be free of Agatha and Autumn Stanton, and would return to the city in control of his life. Return to the misty city of love. The city could be misty or filled with brilliant sunshine, but either way there would be no more love in the heart and soul of Graham Cracker Kimble!

Nine

The next thing Autumn knew Graham was gently shaking her shoulder.

"Autumn," he said, "wake up. We're here."

"What?" She slowly lifted her head. "Oh, I must have fallen asleep. What time is it?"

"A little after ten," he said, opening the car door.

She frowned, then opened her own door and stepped out. Immediately, she wrapped her arms about herself for warmth in the damp, chilly night. The light from the stars and moon could not penetrate the low-hanging fog, and it was pitch black in every direction.

"I've got our gear," Graham said. "Follow me."

"Follow you? I can hardly see you! Goodness it's dark out here."

"The cabin is directly ahead."

"Well, wait a minute here."

"What— Hey, what are you doing?"

"Good, you're wearing a belt," she said, hiking up his sweater. "I'll just hold on to it, and you can venture forth. I intend to let go, though, if you fall in a hole. Lead on, Macduff!" she added, laughing merrily.

Graham looked at her over his shoulder, frowned, then started toward the cabin. Damn, her fingers were warm, he thought. She'd slid them between his belt and his bare skin, and the heat was zinging through his entire body. Actually, he'd expected her to holler her head off because it was so dark and spooky. Dammit, she had such warm fingers!

"You can get your hands out of my pants now," he said gruffly as he set the coats and suitcases on the ground. "I'll unlock the door."

"Okay," she said, slowly withdrawing her fingers. Graham gritted his teeth as tingling sensations feathered up his back. "I hope it's warmer inside," she added.

He pushed the door open, picked up the luggage, and stepped inside with Autumn right behind him.

"Wait here," he said. "I'll go throw the main power switch."

He went back outside, and she squinted into the darkness trying to see anything inside the cabin. All she could discern were vague outlines of furniture.

"Son of a gun," Graham said from behind her. "The electricity isn't working."

"No kidding?" she said. "Now what are we going

to do? It's awfully cold. Is there a fireplace in here, and dry wood?"

"Yeah. Stay put. I'll go into the kitchen and find the oil lamp."

She leaned back against the door as he made his way cautiously forward in the darkness.

"Ow! Dammit!" he yelled an instant later.

"What happened?"

"I whacked my shin on a table. That really hurt!"

"Poor baby," she said, swallowing her laughter.

"Stow it, Stanton," he grumbled.

Graham ran into two more obstacles in his path and cut loose with a string of expletives that made Autumn's eyes widen.

"What a mouth," she muttered under her breath. "That's terrible!"

A few minutes later he returned, carrying a hurricane lamp. Its glow sent flickers of light over his face, and Autumn laughed.

"You look like a mean, crabby pirate," she said. "You swear like one, too."

"Yeah, well, I nearly killed myself. I really don't think it's very funny, Autumn."

"Sorry," she said, but one more bubble of laughter escaped from her lips.

"Hell," he said, hunkering down in front of the fireplace. "All right, let's see here."

The light from the lamp made it possible for Autumn to cross the room with no injury to her person, and she dropped to her knees beside Graham.

"What a beautiful fireplace," she said, glancing upward. "The stones are lovely."

"I gathered them all myself," he said, stacking paper and kindling on the grate.

"I assume you designed this cabin?"

"Yeah. Where're the matches?"

"Here." She handed him the box. "You know, it must be an incredible feeling to start from nothing and create something tangible like this."

"Someone else built it."

"Yes, but it came from your ideas, your imagination. You're very fortunate to have such talent. Some people's dreams get no farther than their hearts."

He turned his head to look at her for a long moment. Suddenly he yelled and dropped the lit match. "I burned my fingers!"

"Oh, dear," she said, and took the box from him. "I'll do it. At the rate you're going, you won't live to see tomorrow."

"Cute."

She lit the paper in several places, and flames leaped upward, licking at the kindling. He stacked a couple of logs on top, and soon the fire was burning steadily, sending warmth and an orange glow out into the room.

"Heavenly," Autumn said.

"I'm hungry," Graham said.

He carried the lamp into the kitchen, and Autumn shifted to sit Indian style on the floor and stared into the flames. A cozy, romantic fire, she thought wistfully, in a quiet cabin in the woods, with just the two of them. She was alone with the man she loved, for all the good it would do her. Darn that Graham Kimble. Why did he have to be so stubborn? She was vaguely aware of Graham banging around in the kitchen as she sat before the fire, nearly hypnotized by the flames. She pushed the distressing thoughts from her mind as the last of the chill ebbed from her body.

Graham reentered the living room and stopped at the sight before him. Beautiful, he thought. The firelight had turned Autumn's hair to gold. She had such a serene expression on her face, and her skin was glowing from the warmth of the fire. She was without a doubt the most beautiful woman he had ever seen.

And so far she'd been a good sport about the lack of electricity, he thought. He'd been the one ranting and raving. For two cents, he'd go throw that circuit breaker because he wanted a big, juicy steak. Well, Autumn would start complaining when she found out all there was to eat were pretzels. But damn, she was lovely in the gentle light of that fire.

"Pretzels," he said gruffly, striding toward her.

"Really? I love pretzels."

"You do?"

"Sure. We'll get awfully thirsty, though."

"Oh. Well, I guess I could dig out a bottle of wine."

"A jug of wine, pretzels, and thou," she said, laughing.

"Mmm." He turned on his heel and left the room. Why in hell was she in such a good mood? he silently fumed. They were in a cabin in the middle of nowhere, with no electricity, food that was frozen solid, and a box of pretzels! She was acting as though she'd just checked into a fancy resort!

He returned with the wine and two glasses, then

settled onto the floor, resting his back against the sofa. He stretched his long legs out in front of him and crossed them at the ankle. Autumn scooted next to him and smiled when he handed her a glass of wine.

"Thank you," she said. "It's so peaceful here, Graham. I could sit here for a week and not move. I'm realizing how long it's been since I've really relaxed. I feel as though I've been studying for my doctorate forever. Oh, sorry. I guess that's not a very popular subject with you."

He smiled slightly. "Not high on my list," he said. "However, I do admire you for going after your degree the way you have. It would have been a lot easier to marry some rich guy and let him support you in the manner you're accustomed to. I respect your drive and intelligence, Autumn, but . . ."

"Yes, I know," she said, sighing. "I blew it when I invented Agatha. I'm so terribly sorry for everything that happened. I wish you'd believe that."

He looked at her quickly, then redirected his attention to the fire. Sorry about everything? he repeated to himself. Sorry they had made love, shared an experience beyond description in its intensity and beauty? Dammit, didn't she have more than ice in her veins? How many men did she give herself to the way she had to him? Hell, why was he worrying about it? This was Autumn, and he didn't like her, not one little bit.

"But you don't believe that I'm sorry, do you?" she went on, staring into her wineglass.

"I believe," he said gruffly, "that it was all a game to you, all of it. You were gathering your data and getting a good laugh out of the deal at the same time. I fell in love with Agatha, you knew that, and it still didn't stop you."

"And I fell in love with you," she whispered.

"I told you not to say that! I wanted Agatha to say those words, and I sure as hell don't want to hear them from you! What I can't figure out is why you insist on saying them at all. You know the rules of the game. Declarations of love aren't necessary in the world of casual sex and one-night stands."

"I don't have casual sex and one-night stands!" she said, her voice rising. "How dare you stick a label like that on me. You have no idea what you're talking about."

"Oh, no? You do recall that we made love, don't you, Autumn? That *was* me in your bed. It was nothing more to you than a quick tumble to collect data!"

"That's not true!"

"Ha!" He drained his glass.

"Oh, you sit there so smug with your judgments, accusations, and your preachings about honesty. Honesty? My big toe, Kimble! You lied to Agatha right from the beginning!"

"What? You're crazy."

"No, I'm not. You told her that you loved her just the way she was. Then you nearly tripped over your feet in your rush to change her. First it was her hair, then her clothes. For her comfort, you said. Bull. It was for you, and you know it. You were going to show her off like a prize, strut your stuff in front of other men. I've seen the way you look at me, Graham. You enjoy beautiful women, just like the next guy. You were the one playing games with

Agatha, and if she were real, you'd owe her an apology!"

He opened his mouth, then shut it and shook his head. He stared at the ceiling for a long moment before he spoke.

"You're right," he said quietly. "I was trying to change Agatha. I saw her hidden beauty, and made up my mind to bring it to the surface. I kidded myself for a while by pretending I was doing it for her. But I wasn't. I was being totally selfish, wanted everything my way. Agatha's values and outlooks were perfect. Her appearance I could fix. Hell, I'm a louse."

"No, you're not. You're a human being. I don't think there's anything wrong with wrapping a gift in pretty trimmings instead of plain brown paper. We're all products of our egos, and a society that plays on those egos."

"You sound like a shrink."

"I hope so," she said, smiling. "Otherwise, I've wasted a lot of time studying my little heart out."

"Well, those jokers better accept your dissertations, no questions asked. You deserve that degree."

"Thank you, Graham."

Their eyes met and held in a gaze that stopped time. Orange lights from the fire danced across their faces. Their heartbeats quickened as growing desire was reflected in eyes of emerald green and fudge-dark brown. They didn't move. They hardly breathed. They just sat staring at each other, as awareness heightened and passions were rekindled.

"Autumn," Graham finally said, his voice hoarse, "don't do this to me."

Tears sprang to Autumn's eyes, and she turned her head to hide them. It was no use, she thought miserably. Graham was too big, too tough; the walls he'd constructed around himself were too high. There was nothing she could say or do that would change his opinion of her. She had loved and lost. Whoever had said it was better than never having loved at all didn't know how badly the losing hurt.

"Autumn," he said, "are you crying?"

"No. Of course not. I'm very tired, Graham. I'd like to go to bed. I assume there're beds in this place?"

"Yes, two bedrooms upstairs. This is an A-frame like the one I'm designing for Fisher. He accepted my preliminary ideas, by the way. You prepared excellent notes on that site visit."

"Agatha wrote up those notes. And Agatha typed perfect reports, and made delicious coffee." Autumn stood up. "It was your wonderful Agatha who shared her dream with you of combining a career with a family, and—" she stopped speaking as tears spilled over onto her cheeks. "And she was the one you made love to. Agatha was willing to dress any way that pleased you, and lived for the moment you took her into your arms."

"Autumn, don't cry," Graham said, getting to his feet and reaching for her.

"Don't touch me," she said, stepping back. "I give up, Graham. You win, I lose. But damn you, I'm going to say this once more. The only difference between Agatha and me was our appearance!

That's all. Everything else was the same, don't you understand? She didn't tell you that she loved you because I wouldn't allow her to be a part of our lives. Those words were mine to say. Mine! I love you, Graham—but I think I hate you, too!"

"Autumn—"

"Shut up. Just shut up! I've heard enough of your accusations and cutting remarks, and I won't listen to any more. Believe what you will about me, because I don't care. You want me and Agatha out of your life? Fine, we're gone. She never existed, and I'm back in the fast lane, bed-hopping all over San Francisco. There's no one here for you, Graham. You're free, just like you wanted to be!"

"No!"

"May I go upstairs now?" she asked with biting formality. "I'd like to get some sleep."

"It'll be cold up there. Don't move, okay? I'll be right back."

"Where are you going?"

"Just stand right there," he said, and dashed outside.

"Why not?" she mumbled, throwing up her hands. Well, that had been quite a performance she'd put on. She'd bared her soul and cried in front of Graham. Where was her sense of pride, her dignity? Smashed to smithereens along with her heart, that's where. She wanted to go home. She wanted to leave this place and Graham Kimble, and go home.

"Okay," he said, running back in and slamming the door. "There." He turned on a lamp. "And the heat just kicked in. It'll be warm in here in a few minutes."

"How did you suddenly produce electricity?"

"I lied about that, Autumn. I never threw the main power switch."

"Why?"

"Because I was sure you would moan and groan about the inconvenience; then I'd have more evidence that you were totally opposite from Agatha. But you were wonderful, even about the pretzels. I'm sorry. It was a rotten thing to do."

"Gathering data, were you, Graham?" she said, a sharp edge to her voice. "My, my, how interesting. Are we even now? Yes, I think we are. And that's the end of it."

"Autumn, listen to me for a minute."

"No. No more." She walked across the room and picked up her suitcase. "Which bedroom do you prefer to use?"

"It doesn't matter. Autumn, I want to talk to you!"

"Well, frankly, my dear," she said, tossing her head, "I really don't give a damn."

"This is not the time to be funny!"

"It's either that or shoot you!" she said, stomping up the stairs. "I swear I have cried my last tears because of you. Good night! No, it's not. It's the worst night of my life!"

"But—dammit!" he muttered as she slammed the bedroom door behind her. He flopped down on the sofa, running his hand over the back of his neck. "You're an idiot, Kimble," he said to the fire. "A fool, a sleazeball, and a jerk!"

And he was in love with Autumn Stanton.

As she had stood before him, tears streaming down her face, he'd been filled with a greater joy than he had ever known. Every word she'd said had been the truth, he realized. She had spoken from her heart, her soul. She loved him.

He allowed her declaration of love to wash over him, warming him like rich brandy, extinguishing the cold chill of loneliness. It wasn't wrong, he decided, to admit he had loved Agatha, for Agatha was Autumn, one and the same. Autumn wanted a family as well as her career. Autumn believed in the same things he did, shared his dreams. And it had been Autumn he had made love with.

Yes, he was very deeply in love with Autumn.

And she would probably never speak to him again for as long as she lived.

There was no excuse for the things he'd said, the accusations he'd hurled at her. He was definitely a louse. So, now what? How did he make amends, convince her he was sincerely sorry, had seen the light, the error of his ways?

"What in the hell am I going to do?" he muttered. Was it supposed to rain? he wondered. A thunderstorm would be great. A terrific, noisy, scary thunderstorm. Autumn would wake up screaming in fright, and he'd race to her rescue, pulling her into his strong, comforting arms. She'd cling to him, he'd kiss away her fears, then . . . Then she'd toss him out of the room!

He was too tired to think straight, he decided, pushing himself to his feet. Maybe a good night's sleep would refresh his brain and produce a brilliant idea as to how he was going to convince Autumn that he loved her and wanted to marry her.

He set a screen in front of the fireplace, picked

up his suitcase, turned off the light, and slowly climbed the stairs. He stopped outside Autumn's room and stared at the closed door, willing it to open and bring Autumn leaping into his arms.

"Probably with a machete in her hand," he said, and walked into the other bedroom.

Autumn lay wide awake in the bed, the blankets pulled up to her chin. She'd heard Graham come up the stairs and was sure he had stopped outside her door. She'd tensed, waiting to see if he'd come in, then couldn't decide if she was relieved or disappointed when he walked away.

She was thinking in circles and she knew it. Love was, without a doubt, a very complex and confusing emotion. It was also, to use Graham's favorite word, honest, for it resided in the most essential, true part of herself. How much, she realized, she had learned about herself since falling in love with Graham Kimble.

She had always taken her looks for granted, never questioning her ability to walk among the affluent and beautiful and be accepted. Agatha had shown her that some are not so blessed with natural beauty. But they, too, would be loved by the right person at the right time. The inner being was, indeed, far more important than the outer trappings. It was a lesson well learned, and Autumn was ashamed to think she had discovered the knowledge so late in her life.

She closed her eyes and tried to sleep, but images of herself, Agatha, and Graham filled her mind. She groaned, and then inspiration struck.

The way things had been going, Agatha would have become Autumn eventually. What if she gave Graham and Agatha another chance?

She rolled over onto her stomach, punched her pillow, pretended it was Graham's nose and punched it again. "Okay, Kimble," she said decisively, "gear up, because the final whistle hasn't been blown after all!" Then she snuggled into a comfortable position. A few minutes later she drifted off to sleep. And she was smiling.

Ten

With sunlight dancing across her face, Autumn opened her eyes and wondered where she was. Then she remembered she was in Graham's cabin and sat bolt upright in bed, wide awake.

It was seven A.M. and, she thought dramatically, the first day of the rest of her life, or however that saying went.

She glanced around the room, having paid little attention to the decor the previous night, and decided immediately that it was charming. The furniture was Early American, and there was a patchwork quilt on the bed. She vaguely remembered that the living room had also been done in the same motif, a fact she'd been unaware of until Graham had made his magnanimous gesture of turning on the electricity. Personally, she'd preferred sitting in the dark in the warm glow of the fire.

A steady thudding noise reached her ears, and she slid off the bed and walked to the window. Brushing back the gingham curtains, she looked out, and her breath caught in her throat. Graham was out back chopping wood. His jeans rode low on his hips and his bare back, glistening with perspiration, rippled with muscles at every swing of the axe.

He was so beautiful, she thought once again. So big and strong, perfectly proportioned. He was the epitome of masculinity, and by golly, she was his woman!

"Quit gawking at him, Autumn," she told herself firmly. "You have important things to do!"

She tapped a finger against her chin and considered the number of logs Graham obviously intended to chop into smaller pieces. She had plenty of time. She hoped. But there were so many variables to consider. Could she dash outside without Graham seeing or hearing her? Were his car keys in the cabin or, heaven forbid, in his pocket? And most important, was what she was seeking still in the trunk of his car?

She sent a mental message to Graham to stay at his chore until it was completed, then hiked up her nightgown and ran from the room. After hurrying down the stairs, she looked around frantically for Graham's car keys.

"Hooray!" she whispered when she spotted them on the end table.

Once outside she moved cautiously, immediately regretting that she had not put on her shoes. She carefully opened the trunk, willing it not to make a sound. Hardly breathing, she peered inside.

They were there!

The awful mustard-colored dress and ugly shoes that had gotten soaked in the rain were still in the trunk. She snatched up her treasures, closed the trunk with a quiet click, and ran for the house. Safely back inside her room, she leaned against the door and let out a rush of air. A quick look out the window assured her that Graham, beautiful, bare-chested Graham, was still busy at his task.

After her shower she shook out the crumpled dress. It was badly wrinkled, but fairly clean and completely dry. It was also as hideous as she remembered.

Fifteen minutes later, Agatha Stanton descended the stairs.

In her awful dress, black oxfords, her hair in a lopsided bun, and her face devoid of makeup, Agatha was very much on the scene. She walked into the kitchen, poured herself a cup of coffee, and sat down at the table. Then, with her heart beating wildly and butterflies swooshing through her stomach, she waited.

Ten long, agonizing minutes later, Graham came through the back door. He was mopping his face with his T-shirt, then he ran it over his chest and looked up, directly at her.

His entire body stiffened so suddenly that Autumn mused irrationally that it was a wonder all his joints hadn't locked. His eyes widened. His mouth dropped open.

"Hello, Graham," she said, delighted that her

voice was steady. "You've certainly been working hard this morning."

"Agatha?" he asked, moving forward tentatively and sinking onto the chair opposite her. "No. No, there is no Agatha. Autumn, why are you being Agatha?"

"It's really very simple. We're moving the clock back, Graham."

"We are?"

"Oh, yes. It's the perfect solution to solving the problems between us."

"It is?"

"Certainly. Shall I proceed?"

"Please do," he said. He leaned back in his chair, crossed his arms over his bare chest, and frowned.

"Even as I sit here before you as Agatha, you know that I am Autumn, right? Right. Because there is no Agatha. However, you have a mental block about Autumn. Due to your experiences, you have a preconceived opinion about women who are attractive. Therefore, when I speak to you as Autumn you refuse to believe me or listen, really listen, to what I'm saying."

"Autumn, I—"

"The floor is mine, Mr. Kimble."

"Sorry," he said, suppressing a smile. "Carry on."

"So!" she said, pointing a finger in the air. "I am reentering your life, after having exited it last night, as Autumn Stanton, but I'm here without the trimmings. I'm in a condition you seem more willing to accept, as was proven by your immediate attraction to Agatha. Everything I say and do will be honest, and there's nothing about me to distract you from discovering who and what Autumn Stanton is."

"I see," he said, nodding. "Everything you say and do will be totally honest?"

"Absolutely. You do, of course, have the option to refuse to cooperate, and may choose to dismiss me from your life." *Oh, Graham, no!* she pleaded silently. *Give us a chance! Please, Graham!*

He stood and walked to the window, bracing his hands on the frame and staring out.

This was nuts! he thought. Everything had fallen into place for him last night. He loved Autumn and wanted to marry her. This plan of hers was crazy, and it was wonderful. She was really something. She was feisty, and determined, and fantastic. He could tell her that now, but he was curious to see how far she'd go with this cuckoo scheme.

"I accept your proposal," he said, turning to face her. "I don't like being accused of having a closed mind. A man can't go through life wondering if he has preconceived, unfair opinions, can he? No, of course, not. Hello, Autumn Stanton." He extended his hand. "I'm Graham Kimble."

She stood slowly and placed her hand in his, gazing up into his eyes.

"Hello, Graham Kimble," she said, her voice hardly above a whisper.

They didn't move as they looked at each other, and the heat from their clasped hands seemed to grow, enveloping both of them, drawing them closer, and kindling embers of desire.

Forget this nonsense, Graham told himself. He wanted to kiss Autumn, hold her, make love to her throughout the entire day. He wanted to tell her that he loved her. But no. It seemed important to her that they start over, erase the past hurts and begin again, so he'd do it her way. And besides, he really was curious as to just what she had in mind.

Autumn firmly told herself not to raise her other hand and sink her fingers into the moist curls on Graham's chest. And not to lean forward and press her lips to his. She inhaled his musky scent, the mingled aromas of soap and sweat, and prayed he couldn't hear the wild beating of her heart.

He cleared his throat and slowly retrieved his hand. "Had breakfast?" he asked.

"What? Oh, no, I haven't, but I really don't care for any."

"Well, I need a shower. Then I think we should go back to the city."

"Why?"

Because he was liable to pick her up and carry her to bed! he thought. "Because it isn't realistic here, Autumn. It's too easy to forget there's a world out there. I think we should begin fresh Monday morning when you report to my office as my secretary." Oh, hell! What a lousy idea. He wanted her so damn much. But he also needed a little space. One thing was for damn sure, though. He wasn't playing this silly game for long.

"Oh. Well, all right," Autumn said, acutely aware of her disappointment. "I'll go pack. By the way, Graham, this is a beautiful home. I really like the way you blended it into the environment. I feel very strongly about preserving the trees and tampering with nature as little as possible."

"You do?"

"Oh, yes. In fact, my father had to bail me out of jail once because I was with a group that was picketing without a permit against a construction firm."

"No kidding?" He grinned at her. "Jail?"

"It wasn't so bad. They plopped us in there just in time for lunch. They had the most delicious orange marmalade. Well, I'll go pack," she said, and left the kitchen, her shoes clumping on the tile.

Graham laughed softly and shook his head. "Oh, Autumn," he said to the empty room, "I do love you so much. Orange marmalade?" And he laughed again.

In less than an hour, Graham turned the key in the ignition of the Ferrari and pulled away from the cabin. Autumn turned to look at the lovely house until it disappeared from view. They drove in silence for the first half hour, Autumn occasionally sticking a loose pin back into her hair. She brushed her hands a few times over the wrinkles in her dress but soon gave up the useless effort.

"When do you think you'll have your dissertation completed?" Graham finally asked.

"In a few weeks. All I have to do is incorporate the last of my notes into it, then have it professionally typed. I've dealt with it too long, and can't bear the thought of typing the thing."

"Then you will have accomplished your goal," he said. And she'd be free. Free to love, live, marry. Marry *him!*

"Yes. Well, that goal, at least," she said. And beyond those were the other dreams, dreams of becoming Graham's wife, growing big with his child, staying by his side for the remainder of her days.

"We all have dreams, Autumn," he said quietly.

She glanced at him, wanting to ask what his dreams were. But she kept silent, telling herself that the questions were his to ask, the discoveries his to make, as she had proposed in her plan. She would force no issues, make no move to convince him of her sincerity. Their futures were in his hands. Was it going to work for them? Would he get to know her, then come to love her? All she could do was wait.

He steered the conversation to lighter topics, asking her about her family, her youthful pranks with Clint. Their mingled laughter echoed through the car, filling it to overflowing. As they drove onto the Golden Gate Bridge, Graham chuckled.

"Do you have any more nifty trivia about this bridge to share?" he asked, smiling.

"Oh, yes. For example, during World War Two the *Queen Elizabeth* steamed into San Francisco as a troop ship. Her topmast cleared the bridge with less than two feet to spare. It was a very tense moment. Unfortunately, the bridge is also known for the suicides that take place. Most of the suicides are men, most go on a Tuesday in May and October. It is believed that the majority climb over the rail on the eastern side, where they can have one last look at the city before they jump."

"Sad, but interesting. All that info you have stored in your head is fascinating, Autumn. I enjoy it."

"Thank you," she said, giving him a warm smile.

In her apartment, he set her suitcase and jacket on the floor just inside the door, then shoved his hands into the pockets of his jeans.

"Well," he said, "I guess I should go." He didn't want to leave.

"Would you like a sandwich?" she asked. Oh, she wished he'd stay!

"No, thank you. Autumn, I apologize for forcing you to go to the cabin, then pulling that adolescent trick with the electricity. I was really at the end of my rope, but that's no excuse for my behavior. I hope you'll forgive me."

"Yes, of course I do."

"I appreciate that. I'll see you Monday morning, all right?"

"All right, Graham, and we'll start fresh, with a clean slate."

"Yeah," he said, placing his hand on the doorknob. He turned to look at her, and their gazes seemed to hold for an eternity. He began to pull his hand free, then hesitated. "Bye," he said, and opened the door and quickly left.

"Bye," she said softly, then picked up her suitcase and walked heavily into the bedroom, her oxfords dragging in the thick carpet.

She unpacked and changed, then fixed herself a sandwich that she ate without tasting.

She should, she supposed as she stared at a spot on the wall, spend the remainder of the weekend working on her dissertation. Yes, that would help pass the hours. The long, lonely hours ahead until she would see Graham again.

*   *   *

Graham ate an apple, a banana, and an orange, then settled onto the sofa in his living room with a bag of potato chips. He was bored. And he missed Autumn. He wanted to march back to her apartment and tell her that he loved her, that Agatha was out of his life forever, and the future was theirs to share.

But no, he decided, maybe it was better this way. He and Autumn did need to put the past behind them, forgive and forget the misunderstandings and the pain they'd caused each other. They'd spend the weekend apart, then view things fresh on Monday. How long he could wait before telling her that he loved her, he didn't know. For now they would talk, share, build a solid foundation for their relationship. On Monday morning his beautiful Autumn would be at the office— Beautiful? Oh, Lord, how long was she going to dress like Agatha?

Graham chuckled. "Well, I asked for it," he said aloud. There had to be a way, he mused, to speed this whole thing up, though. "I've got it!" he said, snapping his fingers and spilling the potato chips. "All right! My genius-level brain is back in action!"

At last Monday arrived and Autumn hurried to the office. She was dressed in a large purple dress with baggy red sleeves and her oxfords. The lopsided bun was in its lopsided place. She had no sooner laid her purse on the desk when Bish entered.

"Hi, Aut— Oh, hell, you're Agatha again! What is going on now?"

"Well, you see—"

"Good morning, all," Graham said.

Autumn and Bish turned to face Graham.

"Good Lord!" Autumn said.

"Cracker?" Bish said incredulously. "Is that you?"

"Yep," he said, appearing very pleased with himself.

Autumn and Bish walked slowly toward him, their gazes sweeping over him, over his enormous striped shirt, plaid Bermuda shorts, dark socks, and tattered tennis shoes. His hair was also parted in the middle and plastered down with water, and he needed a shave.

"Well," he said, smiling broadly, "what do you think?"

"That you're a sick, sick man," Bish said, shaking his head.

"Graham, why are you dressed like that?" Autumn asked, amazed that her voice was working.

"It's very simple," he said. "We agreed to start fresh this morning, on equal footing. You have stripped away the outer wrappings so that I won't be distracted, and I felt it was only fair that I do the same. You've expressed strong feelings for me, Autumn, but how do you know that you're not just physically attracted to me? What about me, the inner person? You said I was guilty of wanting to change Agatha's appearance, and I admitted that guilt. But can you honestly say you haven't been swayed by how I dress, the way I'm built? Answer that one, Ms. Stanton."

"That's it," Bish said, heading for the door. "I've had it. I can't take any more of this. You're both lunatics and you deserve each other. Good-bye, crazy people. It has not been a pleasure knowing you!"

"Well?" Graham said to Autumn as Bish slammed the door shut behind him.

Her gaze swept over him once more from head to toe. She opened her mouth to speak, but laughter erupted, growing louder each time she looked at him.

He frowned. "Knock it off," he said gruffly. "This is serious business here. You're supposed to be talking to me, not falling apart. So, what do you think?"

"I think," she said, smiling warmly, "that you are the dearest, most wonderful man I have ever known. I think—no, I know—that I love you beyond description. You are my love, my life, Graham Kimble. I am Autumn Stanton, have always been Autumn. I want you, your love, our baby. I love you, Graham, with my whole heart. And I will honestly say that at the moment you look like hell!"

"Autumn," he said, grinning at her, "so do you!"

"I know!" she said, and dissolved into laughter again.

He suddenly grew serious. "There's something I have to say to you."

"Yes?" she said, her laughter coming to an abrupt halt as a knot tightened in her stomach.

"I love you," he said quietly.

"Pardon me?" she said, blinking once slowly.

"I love you, Autumn Stanton. You are everything and more than I have ever dreamed, *prayed*, to find in a woman. Will you marry me, Autumn?"

"Oh, Graham, yes!" she said, and flung herself into his arms.

He brought his mouth down hard onto hers as he gathered her tightly to him. Their lips parted, their tongues met, and their passions soared. The kiss was urgent, hungry. It spoke of want, of need, and of commitment to a lifetime together.

"I love you so much," Graham said when he raised his head. "I want to make love to you right now. Let's go to my apartment."

"But you have work to do."

"I'm not sure any of my clients could handle my transformation. I'll call and cancel my appointments."

"Oh, Graham, are we wrong? We do place so much importance on how we look. I'm not comfortable dressed like this. I like feeling pretty, knowing I've enhanced whatever natural beauty I was blessed with. And you do the same thing. Does that make us egotistical?"

"I don't know, I really don't. We are who we are, and we understand each other so well. The thing we have to remember is that our children must have the right to make their own choices. We'll help them, guide them, as they grow within themselves, but the rest will be up to them."

"You'd keep quiet if our daughter was an Agatha?"

"I'd even loan our son these shorts," he said, smiling.

"Oh, Graham, I love you so. Make your calls and let's go home."

* * *

At his apartment, Graham disappeared into the bathroom to shave. Autumn walked into the bedroom and pulled the pins from her hair, combing it free with her fingers. She shed her clothes, and when Graham emerged from the bathroom she faced him without embarrassment. He quickly rid himself of his own clothes, and the splendor of his body made her catch her breath.

"This is as honest as we can get," he said, walking slowly toward her. "We have only ourselves to offer to each other. Our bodies are bare, our hearts, souls, and minds centered on our love. We are man and woman in our purest form."

"And you are beautiful," she whispered.

"So are you, my love."

He pulled her to him and brushed his lips over hers. Then the kiss deepened as his hands roamed over the silken skin of her back, her hips, then up to the sides of her full breasts. She leaned against him, relishing the evidence of his arousal, anticipating the moment they would become one.

He left her only long enough to throw back the covers on the bed, then lifted her onto the cool sheets. He stretched out next to her and began a languorous journey over her eager body with his lips, tongue, and hands. Autumn, too, rediscovered the wonders of him, touching and kissing, igniting his passion to a fever pitch that matched her own.

Their joining was magnificent.

It was the physical and the emotional intertwined. They were a man and woman sharing a ritual as old as time. Their love had given them a greater understanding of their own inner beings, and of the other to whom they clung.

They soared into ecstasy, calling to each other as they shared the rapture of their love.

Later, they lay quietly, contented. Graham laced his fingers with Autumn's and rested their hands on his chest.

"I don't think Bish survived us," he said, laughing softly.

"He knew who I was from the first day. He does business with my father, and had seen my picture at my parents' home."

"No kidding? That louse. He never said a word. I'll have to speak to him about his loyalty to his ole buddy Cracker. Naw, forget it." He rolled on top of her. "Everything worked out perfectly."

"I love you, Graham Kimble," she said, tears glistening in her eyes. "For better, for worse, whatever you're wearing, I love you."

"What *you* wear best," he said, lowering his lips to hers, "is me!"

THE EDITOR'S CORNER

We've got a "Super Seven" heading your way next month. First you'll get our four romances as always during the first week of the month; then on October 15, we'll have **THE SHAMROCK TRINITY** on the racks for you. With these "Super Seven" romances following up our four great LOVESWEPTs this month and coming on the heels of Sharon and Tom Curtis's remarkable **SUNSHINE AND SHADOW**, we hope we've set up a fantastic fall season of reading pleasure for you.

Leading off next month is **STILL WATERS**, LOVE-SWEPT #163, by Kathleen Creighton who made a stunning LOVESWEPT debut with **DELILAH'S WEAKNESS**. **STILL WATERS** is a love story that sparkles with whimsy while proving that old saying "still waters run deep." Maddy Gordon works with troubled children, using puppets in play situations to reach them. Wary and self-protective, she also uses her puppets to fend off people who dare to get too close to her. Nothing, though, can keep Zack London away from her. This forceful, sexy, loving man didn't win Olympic Gold Medals by fading when the going got tough, so he isn't about to be deterred by any obstacle Maddie can put in his path. This is a richly emotional love story that we think you'll long remember.

Barbara Boswell's **WHATEVER IT TAKES,** LOVE-SWEPT #164, works a kind of physical magic on a reader—melting her heart while taking her breath away. When feisty Kelly Malloy is teamed up against her will with irresistible hunk Brant Madison to do a story on illegal babyselling, the words and sparks fly between them. Each has secret, highly emo-

(continued)

tional reasons for being so involved in the subject they are investigating. As those secrets are gradually revealed, along with the plight of the children used in the racket, the intensity of Kelly's and Brant's growing love builds to a fever pitch. Another very special romance from Barbara Boswell!

That delightful duo Adrienne Staff and Sally Goldenbaum bring you a richly emotional, joyous romance in **KEVIN'S STORY,** LOVESWEPT #165. I'm sure many of you remember Kevin Ross who was befriended by Susan Rosten in **WHAT'S A NICE GIRL. . . ?** Kevin is now a successful businessman, seeking a model to be the spokeswoman for his product when gorgeous Suzy Keller sweeps into his life. It's love at first sight, but a love Kevin is determined to sabotage. Suzy isn't about to let that happen though . . . and she sets out to prove it in the most provocative ways possible. He may not be able to hear her passionate whispers, but he'll feel the force of her love every day, in every way!

In **LISTEN FOR THE DRUMMER,** LOVESWEPT #166, Joan Elliott Pickart will keep you chuckling while cheering on the romance of zany Brenna MacPhee and conservative Hunter Emerson. Brenna runs a pet hotel; Hunter runs a business. Brenna lives in a wildly unpredictable world; Hunter has everything in his life organized to a "T," including his wardrobe, composed exclusively of white shirts and dark suits and ties. Despite their differences he's unreasonably mad about the woman . . . especially when he discovers a need in her life as great as the one in his! Be sure not to miss this latest delight from Joan!

I've described **THE SHAMROCK TRINITY** before, but let me whet your appetite a bit more by

(continued)

reminding you that these three interrelated love stories are by Kay Hooper, Iris Johansen, and Fayrene Preston. On the back covers of the books we describe the Delaney brothers as "powerful men . . . rakes and charmers . . . they needed only love to make their lives complete." You'll learn how true those words are to your great pleasure when reading these never-to-be forgotten romances—**RAFE, THE MAVERICK** by Kay Hooper; **YORK, THE RENEGADE** by Iris Johansen; **BURKE, THE KINGPIN** by Fayrene Preston. Be sure to have your bookseller save copies of **THE SHAMROCK TRINITY** for you! We believe that **THE SHAMROCK TRINITY** continues the LOVESWEPT tradition of originality and freshness without sacrificing the beloved romance elements. We hope you'll agree and we will eagerly look forward to your response to this "first" in romance publishing. Enjoy the "Super Seven."

Warm regards,
Sincerely,

Carolyn Nichols

Carolyn Nichols
  Editor
LOVESWEPT
Bantam Books, Inc.
666 Fifth Avenue
New York, NY 10103